A TALE THAT NEEDS TO BE TOLD

Diary of a Wayward Caseworker

by

Lorraine J. Smith

The contents of this work, including, but not limited to, the accuracy of events, people, and places depicted; opinions expressed; permission to use previously published materials included; and any advice given or actions advocated are solely the responsibility of the author, who assumes all liability for said work and indemnifies the publisher against any claims stemming from publication of the work.

All Rights Reserved
Copyright © 2023 by Lorraine J. Smith

No part of this book may be reproduced or transmitted, downloaded, distributed, reverse engineered, or stored in or introduced into any information storage and retrieval system, in any form or by any means, including photocopying and recording, whether electronic or mechanical, now known or hereinafter invented without permission in writing from the publisher.

Dorrance Publishing Co
585 Alpha Drive
Suite 103
Pittsburgh, PA 15238
Visit our website at www.dorrancebookstore.com

ISBN: 979-8-88729-399-8
eISBN: 979-8-88729-899-3

To protect the privacy of certain individuals the names and identifying details have been changed.

This is dedicated to those unsung caseworkers who did their job in spite of others and working conditions.

TABLE OF CONTENTS

Preface .ix
Chapter One 1
Chapter Two 9
Chapter Three 23
Chapter Four 35
Chapter Five 57
Chapter Five, Scene Two 63
Chapter Six 91
Chapter Seven 101

PREFACE

This is out of order, a teaser. Like unwrapping a gift that is a mere clue to the real gift.

What is wrong with me. I didn't even in my recollections of the agency touch on some famous or infamous directors. In the beginning we had a tough policy wonk, reminiscent of Hillary. You might not like her, but you would damn well respect her. Her retirement was a great loss. Followed by two connected, youngish black females.

One I recall only for her choice of semi-sheer, deep, deep vee silk blouses and Sharon-Stone postures. Short-lived, memorable for nothing else.

The other was never even seen by the vast majority of the agency, lasting only a few months also. Most of her time was spent commuting to the Caribbean to see a fiancé, who never materialized. Later she headed a small charitable agency for the homeless that vanished after alleged theft of funds. Followed much later by another appointment to a charity that vaporized after a news release of her being named to head same. A pattern of nepotism? Oh so rampant and much more often at lower levels.

Yet so many worked hard and well. Supporting the old adage that the creme does not rise. But don't judge me harsh or judgmental of staff or clients.

This work is a catharsis, you decide whether truth or fiction.

CHAPTER ONE

OPEN OUR EYES AND LOOK AROUND

Yes, I gave away your hard-earned tax dollars.

No, your aunt didn't get anything when she needed it.

Hence, when meeting some groups of people for the first time, it seemed wiser to say one turned tricks for a living, rather than admit one worked for County Welfare.

Welcome to our world.

So I thought our experience deserved at least the same as a Facebook cat story. I'm thinking a share. So a book, more like a diary, might be the way to do that. In essence I am documenting the laughable, the unbelievable, and the truly heart-rending of our experiences with a chaser of insight to its bureaucracy, for those who like that kind of thing. For those following the far right I must say first, there is no evidence that supports you, but worse,

I don't think you even believe what you say. For those of you so rich, detached from reality, or still believing what your far left or even Marxist professors taught you, please donate this book to the library or burn it as it may offend your tender sensibilities, which, of course is your priority. I, however, have no rich girl's guilt. Hence I can think and speak openly and honestly. But I digress, this is not a political statement, more a diary. Occasionally I need to be stopped, or I go off on a rant. What freedom, but then again this is fiction, isn't it? For those who didn't make the book, that could be a good thing. But, then again, it may mean you were a bit boring, definitely not edgy. Sometimes it's only fate that makes the cut.

We have all been told that words mean something. Or do they?

That being said, let's start right there. It seems common in some environments to start all new administrations or change of directors with a change of language or structure. In these cases someone being paid a ridiculously high salary with no hands-on experience, who further has never truly known, or has chosen to forget, any poor or working-class people, decides the word "welfare" is demeaning and may keep those who are eligible from applying for benefits due to negative connotations of the word "welfare." The Federal Government, the Feds, from whence all big benefits begin at the cost of those who pay taxes, say tsk, tsk, this cannot be. We will change the name to The Department of Human Services, DHS. How wonderful is this as right in the name it says humane. Don't stop there. The whole structure is wrong. We aren't units, we are Teams. We aren't supervisors, we are Team Leaders. Funding for retraining so we may learn how offensive this has been and to change the error of our ways cannot be conducted from the regular agency budgets, so it is necessary to take money from client funding to hire consultants who can train us.

Oh, by the way a niece of a commissioner is temporarily without a job, so it would be more expeditious than the normal Human Resource process to get the job done; this could also be a political stepping stone; you know fluff up that resume. It shouldn't really matter that her only training experience is toilet training her five-year-old. After all, she will maybe go to college someday. So agency employees across the USA get trained. Hundreds of forms, envelopes, etc. are reprinted. Another forest dies, owls live in fear. For instance, there is the Public Assistance Manuals, one volume of which is much longer than *War and Peace*. No, that is a distinct under estimate as with food stamps and day care regulations it's closer to the complete works of Shakespeare.

Notably, when new office furniture was finally purchased, many years later, each worker received a bookcase to store this phenomenon. From time to time it must be reprinted and distributed to caseworkers, supervisors, managers, etc., across the country. Generally, there are just updates printed weekly or monthly to add or delete, generally two months after the changes are already in place. I do hope they learn in the future to do this on recycled paper. Please do not ask how many caseworker, supervisors, etc. actually keep a current PAM. It would be an embarrassing answer, although reasonable as time is not allotted for this. We must, of course, now answer the phone "Department of Human Services," which is followed by frequent hang-ups for maybe two years. It becomes obvious that the clients are confused by the change. Where has the Welfare Department they have come to know, if not trust, gone?

If they actually knew this change may have cost them a decrease in benefit amounts, they really would be mad. So the beat goes on, another bureaucrat needs to tie the name to "jobs" and so another name change, more money spent, and jobs for political hangers-on. So much for lipstick on a pig. The Welfare Department, as I will always know it, opened my eyes and mind. In my life's work I learned far more than I ever learned with my late-in-life formal education. I developed a cop's skepticism, logic, and good-heartedness.

The Welfare Dept. on a day-to-day basis, case-to-case basis is reality, no spin. But, caution, the consultants and rule-makers and shakers have enough spin to keep the public eternally confused.

Sorry, I digressed. Back to my beginning. So I needed a job, took a test, aced it, and months later was called for an interview. I accepted the job as it seemed interesting compared to my accounting and managerial background.

The first two weeks were training with never-ending rules and regulations with little hands on experience. As time went on, the training period extended to two months, still not enough for most. I showed up every day got onto the elevator and escaped coughing and choking in a cloud of Tabu and Ambush cologne, which gratefully is now passé. I quickly learned to not breathe until my floor was reached or to use the stairs. I worked in the downtown office of a large metropolitan county that was predominately white. However, the majority of inner-city and low- or no-income families were black, although that changed with time. The size of families was rather large, often five or more children. This also changed with time, as the client base reflected the general population, i.e., two children average. Also, unlike food-stamp-only recipients, the average client was from a generational welfare family. The exception being, women or men who were going through divorces and recently lost their source of income.

The employees of the department were a mix of black and white, with by far fewer black employees and clients at the offices on the west side of town. This also changed with time, with the employees becoming black or Hispanic, particularly in leadership roles. Although I came from a working-class family and lived my younger years in the city, my later years were in exurbia. The only nonwhite American I ever knew before my working years was the son of a South American doctor of German descent. My first six months were a huge culture shock.

Do not misunderstand me; my family did not have money, but we didn't spend what we didn't have either. My father always worked part-time jobs in addition to his full-time employment. We never took a vacation or had a new car. My parents did not ask for government help and if they had, it would have been with the greatest of humility and gratitude. No, I must correct that statement. I was actually born in the public projects as my mother's first husband died very young and suddenly. This was during WWII and no housing was available. As soon as she married my father upon his return from fighting in the Pacific, they were forced to move out as there was a small income.

I should mention that at the time clients were seen on a walk-in basis. This meant the first two weeks of the month, the busiest, they would come into the waiting room at 8:00 in the morning and wait. And wait. Those of us who worked, may see twenty-five to thirty-some people a day. Some saw as few as two or three people. Not fair, get used to it, this is the Welfare Dept. After two weeks of my own ineptitude, my then supervisor asked me, so who do you know that got you your job. I was beginning to learn how things flowed, so I answered, no one I know got me the job, but someone would help me keep it if I needed them. This was pure bravura, I knew no one. It became very clear to me that there were two classes of welfare recipients. Those who were allegedly poor enough to apply and get benefits and those who got jobs there as payback for political favors or family connections.

Some actually got jobs and worked at them, but this was not the norm. Unfortunately, the public came to think all of us were in this category. To emphasize this, I once called a State Representative in order to express the need for pay raises for caseworkers, as at that time some netted less than clients (if they paid for daycare), he said he would research my info, but couldn't believe I worked there as I spoke too intelligently. I thanked him but let him know that others were intelligent also, we just got lost in the appointees, aka mandatory hires. Actually, I called two State Reps., giving them detailed comparisons of client benefits to caseworkers pay and work-related expenses, both were surprised and did vote in the raises.

CHAPTER TWO

INTRO TO CAST

Please meet some of my coworkers. Let me tell you about Ms. Gospel. Ms. Gospel sang at her church and would practice with other singers somewhere during the working day. It was her lunch hour, of course, but that began late morning and continued until midafternoon, pretty much daily. She would return from lunch, shuffle off to the waiting room, call her client, return to her desk, sit down, and unzip her skirt exposing her girdle which was under great stress from the long lunch. This was probably her second and last client of the day. She worked very hard at not working and was very serious about how she was to be perceived and treated. So of course we laughed about Ms. Gospel. But on days we were really inundated with work, we would bitch about her not working, getting two assignments to our thirty-five or so.

Finally one of the supervisors, tired of our legit complaints, approached Ms. Gospel about not being at her desk most of every day and being totally unproductive. We all sat at our desks glued to the drama as it unfolded. Ms. Gospel, a short old black woman, starts screaming at the very tall, large, black male supervisor who meekly towers over her. She screams, "Fuck with me and you Fuck with George!" Referring to a political figure and a power monger in a local race-based agency. The supervisor immediately turned on his heels returning to his cubicle, not to be seen for the balance of the day. Never again did the subject surface with the exception of Ms. Gospel huffing, puffing, and complaining to anyone within hearing of being so put-upon and having dealt with the problem so well. It might be mentioned that the supervisor who handled this situation so very well went on to become the agency director, after which he went to college in order that he could meet the job requirements. A case of what comes first the chicken or the egg.

Ms. Gospel was by far not the only character. Another favorite was Mr. Cigar, who was married to another agency employee, who, unlike himself, had a history of some competency and a willingness to work. Mr. Cigar was a somewhat good-looking and well-dressed man and very pleased with himself. He would call his client, find out their needs, such as adding a newborn to the case, copy some documents, and deposit this case in either the file cabinet he somehow laid claim to, as no one else had one, or add the case to the piles that encircled his desk. This being done while he puffed away on an over-sized stogie, leaning as far back in his chair as was safe to go, making every effort to emphasize his delusional male superiority. Months later when the same client would come in to change an address, add yet another baby, the record would still be signed out to Mr. Cigar. It would become the next worker's obligation to first find the record as Mr. Cigar isn't going to look for it, then bring the case up to date out of consideration of the client as Mr. Cigar's desk was where work and records went into oblivion. I must confess, in remembering Mr. Cigar, leaning back behind his desk, I get visions of Bill in the infamous cigar incident.

Please don't think we were unkind…well not so much. We had some beloved characters that few could get annoyed with. Ms. Nubile was an extremely lovable, older lady who knew very little and had no common sense. But, she always had a very sweet expression on her face made even more lovable by a wig that was never on quite right. When she had a case for five or more months, it was not from a shrewd case of laziness, but instead because she hadn't decided what to do with it or had forgotten that she even had it.

We were not a ship of fools, but a ship with some fools. Further, in our then-antiquated building, it wasn't easy to get anything done. Everything had to be verified at that time and copied for the record. In a seven-story building, there were only copy machines on the second, sixth, and seventh floors. Also copy machines at that time frequently needed repair, or had jams, etc. So you needed to go to another floor via elevator, which were also old and broken down, or the stairs. The stairs were also not reliable as sometimes rough-looking clients were hanging out or smoking reefer in the stairways. Also at that time, all emergency assistance requests, i.e., clothing orders, mattresses, utility help, had to be signed by both a supervisor and a coordinator. Often they were in meetings, at lunch, using up sick time before retiring, or pandering for a political figure; hence, you had to go to another floor until you found a different coordinator, which required lengthy explanations as you were unknown to them, unless related. Further, if this, God forbid, was duplicate emergency assistance, i.e., for a client being evicted after receiving clothing orders within the last twelve months, you then also needed the associate director's or director's signature. It should also be mentioned that there were only three elevators, with generally one not working. This was not an excuse to fail to copy verifications or get signatures, use the stairs, unsafe as they may be.

There was pretty much no privacy for client or worker. Desks were side by side with a client at either end. Whatever troubles you had were being discussed with a small audience, whether you were talking about unpaid rent or baby daddy. Workers also had no amenities. Bathrooms were shared by the public, which could be awfully nasty as some clients were homeless or just unclean. Toilet paper was often absent in all stalls as food stamps did not cover non-food items and the check usually went to rent, so TP was often stolen. Further intentionally fouling bathrooms and elevators were sometimes responses to not getting all or some of what they asked.

Public image of how tax dollars were spent was extremely important and applied to a fault. We could not even be provided coffee or tea at all day meetings or trainings. Nor did we rate significant security. There were maybe three to four guards for a multi-floor building with hundreds if not thousands of people present per day. These guards were armed only with scowls as weapons. They generally responded too late if at all.

Let me share my own personal experience. After going to the first floor to get a signature or some other errand, I got onto a rather full elevator, as that was usually safest, an empty elevator anyone could jump on at the last minute. These elevators were decades old and broke down frequently. You could end up stuck with a gentleman, or woman, with a propensity to assault or with strange sexual proclivities for an extended period of time. So I'm on the full elevator with all black riders and my white self, I'm in the front corner when a tall evil-looking dude turns sideways and I feel something stuck in my hip that was not a gun. So I shoved him. He says shove me again and I'd just as soon kill you as not for no other reason than you're white.

Not a sound is made by anyone, not even the big ox security guard that happens to be standing next to him. At the next floor I get off, as does the security guard, who disappeared and never again looked me straight in the eye, and we go in opposite directions. I take the stairs the rest of the way to my floor and was very shaken up. I go to my supervisor, letting her know what has transpired. I was further upset to be told, "get used to it; it goes with the territory." In other words, "little white suburban girl, you are out of your element and toughen up or leave." Nothing, of course, is even said to security.

As years went by, this did change, and by the time I retired, we did have more and more able and—surprise, surprise—armed security. It should also be said that at that point in time the biggest incidence of conflict was in the waiting rooms. By mid or late day sometimes clients, generally women, got in physical fights due to comments back and forth during their extended waits for service.

Yet another client fiasco was abandoned children, generally out of total frustration, rarely planned. This meant waiting for Social Services to come and get the kids. Generally it was just a last-ditch verbal threat that could be deescalated by adept workers. Also letting client know they can't just pop back in and pick the kids back up.

I should also mention at that time there was no SSI, (Supplemental Security Income), which is now for the aged and disabled with no or insufficient work history for Social Security, (SSA or

SSD}. There was instead Aid For the Aged, (AFA). So we took care of their dollars, benefits, in addition to medical and food stamps. A few years later the Social Security Administration took on the cash benefits.

I should also mention that not long after leaving that horrific building it was updated with large windows throughout that opened by tilting out, along with a paint job and other amenities. It was then taken over by the Justice Department to be used as a County Jail. Interesting to think it had to be improved upon to meet minimum standards for the common criminal, but was good enough for welfare employees and recipients. The tilt-out windows were appreciated by those remitted, as there were no bars, and it was a knotted sheet or two to street level for most escapees. Quite entertaining. This, of course, precipitated a need for a new welfare office. The building was named after a County Commissioner, who went on to hold, for a long time, a high State Office. Can you say Golden Parachute? Personally, I knew of nothing that warranted either, nor did anyone else. At a later time, I came to know one of his ladies. She, interestingly, left based on disability, mental. She was very entertaining although no work was to be expected of her.

Moving on, now that I have acquainted you with some of our more endearing or more notorious coworkers, let me share with you some vignettes of specific or typical clients, all who shall remain anonymous. I will never forget the older woman, who was very charismatic, who came for her periodic reapplication. In doing so she reported her husband was getting out of prison and returning to the home. She let me know that at least she wasn't worried about having any more babies as he had been in prison so long that he no longer liked women, at least in, you know, that way. We both had a good laugh over that. She was precious and very helpful in expanding my knowledge of life.

Typical of some other mothers, who were perhaps too doting or not strict enough, we had a number of mothers who had several adult sons at home who didn't work or go to school, in fact never graduated from high school. They just aged out of the education system. Today we would probably think they were just a bunch of thugs, and a few were, but many were just either a bit slow or not encouraged enough, some had old-school mothers who assumed there would be no opportunities. The thugs used their, what was called General Assistance, to show as a source of income, $100 per month, when the cops picked them up as a matter of explanation to how they got on with life, i.e., of course they didn't need crime to meet the rent. This program existed only in two states and was discontinued maybe thirty years ago. At that time there were no creditable work requirements, only a few employees to fill out forms and pile them in a room, literally, never to be accessed again. Fifteen years later, there was an actual Jobs department who filled out a couple computer screens, and forms and sorted them before putting them in piles in a room.

For which they were richly rewarded and probably promoted… but more of that later.

As time went on with the younger women, one noticed a pattern of the wiser ones not getting pregnant again, but returning to school. The others seemed to have a pattern of too many baby daddies with every one serving big time in the state prisons. Why do so many women like the bad guys best? Another pattern was ladies of the night coming in still in work apparel, who still needed checks, food stamps, medical to supplement their seldom-stated earnings. In one case, a very attractive young lady sat down at my desk. Her blouse had buttons but none were being used, nor did she have on underwear. So, one very long, thin boob fell out of her blouse. I started laughing and let her know that if she didn't button up a little, my desk mate would soon be back and we would start giggling and never stop long enough to get her case finished. She laughed and buttoned up.

This also reminds me of another caseworker who after a period of time seemed to have a preponderance of repeat clients who were young and very attractive in a somewhat sexual manner. They usually were approved for a lot of clothing and rent orders and the like and spent a long time at his desk. They all asked for him by name (at that time we were supposed to see clients by rotation, not by assigned caseloads). After a period of time, this pattern was noticed and ceased for a time. There was also a supervisor who seemed to have the same pattern of young ladies who needed to see him in his office for special help. Men can be so helpful.

Please understand that this was not the Welfare Dept. of the fifties, when people couldn't own a TV. Also, it was never true a person could not own a house that they lived in as a primary residence, with the exception of nursing home clients. Some of the "less than in true need" clients came in with more real bling and designer bags, shoes, and clothes than the vast majority of us employees could afford, boyfriend could buy anything they liked, they just never paid the rent. Yet, the dollar amount received for ADC was very small and generally included Medicaid for mama and kids with food stamps, and occasional emergency assistance.

People could also go to charitable organizations for a hot meal, a few bags of groceries at the end of the month, or clothing and household items. When you referred clients to these sites and they turned up their noses, you knew the need wasn't really there. Also important to know was that stepfathers were not financially responsible for their stepchildren (this has changed to a large degree), so it was possible for many clients with new spouses to live well to very well, along with their children, and simply not receive food stamps. At that time we also didn't get information on new jobs or other income, assets, etc., until maybe two to three years later. Investigation and overpayments were the exception, not the rule. But when the welfare system went to direct computer input, feedback was received in ten days or so on assets, earnings, and other goodies. This made closings and recoupments more common. On the clients behalf, establishing paternity became both a requirement and a blessing, finding absent parents and their earnings. This was free, no attorney fees necessary, a godsend for moms, some dads, and many grandparents who had custody. This wasn't truly effective until about 1998 when there became agreements across state lines. I'm sure this was a major loss of income for divorce attorneys.

There was also a man, who perhaps was a few IQ points short of average, who took care of things such as in-house mail delivery. This person had a women's shoe fetish. If one was at all appealing and wore stylish shoes, better not leave them at work because they would come up missing. Later to be found some day was his 40-plus pair stash of ladies shoes. He also followed some young ladies like a too-close puppy, which eventually lead to a "no-no don't do that" talking to. He probably was harmless. Not true of all our questionable employees.

Something else I would like the time to make clear, as it is often spoken of as the reason poor women do not marry or live with the father of their children. Men can live with their children and get assistance for all if they have a whisper of a work history. Many race baiters and other proponents of the poor claim this is the reason men don't live with their families; 1) They do, 2) If they had a smidgen of a work history in the last four years or so their families could get more money, 3) This is a known fact in the welfare community. So, the reason men do not live with their families has more to do with abuse, alcohol, another woman, another man, avoiding an outstanding warrant, etc. Don't even tell me the poor are not aware of this possibility for payment as the average long-time food stamp, Medicaid, or ADC recipient knows the regulations better than some workers. This is what they talk about at the Laundromat, just as working people talk about politics that affect them.

What is more likely is that Daddy, or one of them, does live with the family. But as he does work and perhaps makes a good living, Mommy can supplement that with the ADC check and food stamps for her and the kids. Until the last decade or so we didn't have cooperation or access to child support records, so this double income would go on for all that asked. Now, not so much, unless Daddy is self-employed and lies about income to IRS also. This is further complicated when Daddy hops around from family to family. It is ever so common for Daddy not to live with the kids or Mommy and in fact they never see him, but Mommy again gets pregnant with another of his babies. So much happens by airborne viruses.

Another cultural difference from chronic welfare people and temporary recipients is the openness with which they discuss this father and that father in front of the children. The temporary recipients are also likely to be embarrassed and hesitant to discuss anything related to past sexual activity, so 1950s and so refreshing.

For those new to the system or new to multiple daddies, they ask to discuss without child present. Makes sense, after all if not the child is preordained to believe multiple-daddy situation and/or daddy not in household is the norm. But these observations probably make me a far-right elitist, which has become a euphemism for "real."

So we have clarified that one needs be either truly poor or truly evasive to receive anywhere from a pittance to a floodgate of benefits. Now to be fair, I would not call most clients liars. It's just that for many, when you tell the government a lie it doesn't count. Now with all the white collar crime and the lack of veracity in Congress and those who wax presidential, can we see they may have just learned this from their so-called betters. But let us not be too distressed about fraud and daddies not paying support, etc. As time went on record sharing with IRS, child support, workmen's comp (for daddies with the bad back), and unemployment, became readily available. Generally, the mothers would say the baby daddy does support the children, "He buys the diapers," also toys and sometimes comes to visit the kids, babysitting services as needed was very well provided. Unfortunately mommies still had a habit of the yen for the exciting daddies, with expensive tattoos, lots of gold jewelry, willingness to share their drugs and sexually transmitted diseases, who were not as smart as the local cops and ended up doing big time. Worse there are those nasty conjugal visits. Another legal excuse.

I almost neglected to tell you about the coordinator's secretary. Lovely lady, sweet as anything. Grew a garden of indoor plants, even a tree, anyone would be proud of, except it took much of her working day to water, trim, and rotate her plants to get the best sun in her office. She had a philodendron plant that encircled her cubicle. Even more time-consuming was the hand sewing and tailoring she did at her desk to complete the tuxedos and gowns she was making for a wedding with many attendants. What a talented woman. Just don't ask her to type something when she's in the middle of a seam.

CHAPTER THREE

ACT ONE

Next, for less than a year, I worked in a unit that handled strikes (lockouts), large layoffs (i.e. teachers, auto companies, teamsters), and refugees. In some cases, such as the teachers strike, we worked long days, in my case ten or eleven hours, still using the three-ply paper system. My hands by the end of the day wouldn't let loose of the pen and had a painful blister/callous blooming, but I stayed to help the supervisor sign off on the cases. We also had the worst of sites provided, a "too dark to see properly" auditorium, and off-site bathrooms; yes go elsewhere and ask to use their bathrooms. It is time to be reminded that we had those good government jobs with all the benefits. Please keep in mind few teachers applied, especially after they found out their income was averaged for the year as they were under contracts. Most applying were lunch aides, classroom aides, etc.

Aside from this, they were the rudest, most demanding large group we dealt with while I was in that unit. Please withhold your claim that educators, and their cohorts are the salt of the earth. We obviously dealt with none you know. By contrast, the nicest large group were the teamsters. Only a few of them were eligible, yet they thanked us for our time, apologized for taking our time, and provided coffee and pastry (a first). It was either work, work, work, or sit idly waiting for a refugee to show up to apply or reapply.

This was my first experience with refugees. As time went on, I became an acknowledged expert on the refugee and asylee versus immigrant regulations.

To be a refugee you must come from a country acknowledged by Immigration as a country with political strife that threatens all or specific groups who remain there. Hence, you are seeking refuge. Usually the Public Assistance Manual (PAM) will list those countries and may have certain rules or benefits that apply to them. Asylees are those who apply for help through the embassies abroad and if granted can come to this country and be treated similarly to a refugee, or they can walk or fly across our border and request refuge. These two categories are eligible for special benefits that US born childless citizens are not. They can get a small cash assistance, food stamps, Medical for eighteen (18) months. This is not true for immigrants. Immigrants are those who waited in line until their number came up to be eligible for entering this country. Further, they must have sponsors, who must show ability to support them for five years. They are not eligible for any assistance during that five-year period.

Also important to know that, at least for a great many years, it was necessary for the citizen, immigrant, refugee, etc., to prove their status. If they claimed no decision was made yet or they lost their papers they had to be sent back to immigration (which would never happen). Any attempt to call immigration would put you on a twenty-minute loop of prompts followed by a certain disconnect. I once was so irritated by this phone contact situation that I called the local congressional representative's office. The response was that they had the same problems with immigration and had made their own complaints with hopefully the appropriate people to no avail. Also note the Welfare Dept. was not permitted to make referrals back to immigration on illegals when they were known to be so. To be clear, illegals are not asylees or refugees. Keep in mind, I believe I only saw one illegal in my time as a caseworker, as most illegals steer clear of any government offices. For FOX News, let me report that in twenty-five years as an agency employee, I knowingly saw one illegal. You see, receiving benefits means they probably will not get refugee approval. More to the point, most illegals are scared to death that they will be picked up on the spot.

Sounds like things never change. Reflections of today's border problems.

Hence, when politicians and talking heads compare refugees to some of our forefathers they may well be wrong. If your forefathers came here early enough there were no requirements, but in the early twentieth century, that changed. There was also no or slim help. Perhaps a church or other charity may give a very small amount of help, soup kitchens were the reality. But there was no government help, thus no reasonable comparison. Maybe an Orphan Train to a farmer needing free labor, or the rare caring family.

Later it became necessary to wait until your number came up in the imposed quotas and hope your planned sponsors were still willing and able to help. I know my family helped sponsor a family and another relative did likewise. At that time that was the thing to do. So references to our forefathers as compared to present day refugees may well be very wrong.

Basically, the refugee and immigrant regulations are not a blip on a page in a manual, but a chapter of the Public Assistance Manual (P.A.M.). Also, as is true for so much, certain church groups, by religious order or ecumenically, are a huge resource for refugees and asylees. They "sponsor" many groups, which is not to be confused with the Immigration Department's definition of sponsorship. These charities generally help with a few months' rent, some clothing, and housing items. Then they make an appointment for them with the local welfare office for food stamps, cash aid, and Medicaid. They can generally receive the cash and Medicaid for eighteen months (18), unless, based on age or disability, they are further eligible.

As the Iron Curtain came down, a new common occurrence became obvious to those who see patterns. Not to be cruel, just objective, many countries (ex. Romania, and other Eastern European countries) let their asylees leave more readily when they had long-term health concerns or short-term costly ones, i.e., such as leukemias, mental illness, histories of violence, etc. Further, some of these same countries that provide free medical care, free college educations, etc., may require that these benefits be repaid in cash before being able to leave the country. So, alas, they become our taxpayer expenses. Wouldn't it be nice if, on benefit-related issues, questions be posed on the 1040 form so people could put their money where their mouth is, such as, would you willingly pay 5 percent or so additional in taxes to cover refugee expenses? Would you willingly pay 5 percent additional in taxes to continue the expansion of food stamp benefits? I am sure you get my concept; it is also unlimited. Why not medical, infrastructure, etc.?

Also, before you become too touchy, feely about refugees, please keep in mind the first ones out of a situation generally have beaucoup dollars, bhat, ruples, or blocks of gold. The later ones are the "boat people." So temper your humanity as the refugees and asylees of the world may own us one day with the gold and ambition they bring and invest in family businesses. It must be said that in my significant experience with Asian immigrants after their initial years in this country, they have enough ambition and gratitude for the help they have received that seldom do they receive further assistance unless it is Medicaid for the elderly. Of course, with years worked, they will receive Social Security and Medicare, but it should be clear that that is a self-paid insurance program, not a so-called entitlement. The word *entitlement* should never have come into usage. Welfare really more properly expresses what it is. No one comes into this world entitled to pretty much anything.

There are other groups that this can be said of. The Jews for one (they usually have their own welfare institutions). More will be said later of various refugee groups. But keep in mind that asylees must come from countries that Immigration recognizes as countries of political strife that threatens the lives of some or all its citizens.

I personally had experience with the Haitians, Vietnamese, Cambodians, and Laotians. Later this unit was abolished and the refugees were handled by regular case assignment methods. Later I had experience with the Poles, Russians, and other Eastern Bloc Countries. Generally speaking, those coming from communist countries, all had a sense of government entitlement and told you so. Remember they came from communist countries, where this was the norm. But they usually picked up on the joy of private enterprise and did not remain on the welfare rolls interminably. An interesting pattern of many refugees when caught in a lie... there was no embarrassment, but simply anger that they had been caught. If you asked did they lie to their government at home, they would be very offended and let you know, of course not. Obviously they maintained their home soil loyalties, which we hope over a lifetime would change.

Another general group were the Middle-Easterners. The Saudis, etc. were generally very polite, but had been schooled in working the system. Usually they remained intact families with the husband working the minimum hours at the minimum rate to make them eligible for a small amount of cash assistance, and therefore food stamps and most importantly, medical. They generally worked for the same independent grocery stores, Sal's, who assisted them in emigrating. This also helped the stores as they had no need to provide medical, a quid pro quo, and they had cheap dependable labor. Yet so many lived in areas that we could not afford to live, maybe many had family money. All that looks up front and honest is not. Let it be said that they were a regular immigration machine.

Now the Palestinians were a totally different story. They were asylees. They tended to come in and loudly and aggressively demanded assistance. When they were told no, they became very argumentative. The women also were demanding, whereas the Saudi women generally let the husbands handle any questions. It should also be noted that many of the Saudis lived in homes and neighborhoods that few of the employees could ever afford. How does that happen on $200.00 per week? I will let your imagination work that out. Now for those who will scream racism or stereotyping, I will scream back sociological observation and conclusion. Smoke that.

At some point in my career, there was a huge food-stamp-fraud case that sent several owners of small grocery stores, owned by Middle-Easterners, to prison for big-time food-stamp fraud. Generally, for buying food stamps for maybe 50 percent of the face value. This went on for years before fraud charges were brought. That was when food stamps were paper issued, now they are called, SNAP, and are loaded onto a card resembling a credit card, less open to fraud, but still some do manage some fraud.

I'm sorry if I had to bore you with the refugee issues, but every time in the past several years a television personality would go off on a factless tirade on refugees getting beaucoup dollars in food stamps and medical benefits I wanted to scream as I already said they don't want to be seen at government offices. I believe many of these personalities get their info from the backs of cereal boxes or other learning tools within their capacities. If you think I'm being a bleeding heart on refugees, so be it. I just would like TV personalities who make boatloads of money to research for a minute before opining. I'm not sure how I really feel about it, just find it fascinating that it seems that "Game of Thrones" wall seemed to generate a passion for the need of walls. Seemingly, many have forgotten there are planes and boats and no need for a visa to enter from many countries, although overstaying visas is often mentioned. Just come visit Auntie and stay, who will know?

For those who believe there are children starving in the USA, this may be the reason, mama sold the food stamps so she could by cigarettes, booze, or drugs for herself, and baby daddy. If you think… well, Social Services should step in, they can only do so in the most extreme situations. That's a whole story on its own. So basically children only go hungry in the USA if there is neglect, the government cannot fix everything. But to their credit they do try. This is the reason that inner-city schools have free breakfast as well as lunch and even things set up for summer vacations. Where there is neglect, dinner may be a bag of chips. Still far better than almost anywhere else in this world. Better would be to put children's rights on a higher footing compared to parental rights. Little stories will pop up that I either knew of or was more directly involved in as we move along that speak to the abuse or neglect issue. In the meantime if you suspect neglect or abuse, call your local social services department, anonymously works. If you do not, you are part of the problem.

I must digress as I failed to tell you about a most important character. We called him Cool Breeze, as he floated in and out of the office fluidly and frequently. He was reminiscent of a study that showed black males as likely to hang on corners and discuss their education ambitions unlike white males who likely talked about lack of jobs and lack of ambitions. Perhaps the person who conducted the study spoke to Cool Breeze. Cool Breeze was a caseworker that knew little to nothing, often incorrectly. No clue was needed as to how he got into the position. He often left the floor to make a move on an ongoing chess game—code words to smoke a joint in the parking lot. But most importantly he was working on his PhD.

However, he would never mention that it was at one basket-weaving class at a time and that he had yet to get so much as an associate degree from a community college, even though he was well into his forties. More importantly, he did present himself as the professorial type as he always wore a tweed jacket and carried, if not smoked, a meerschaum pipe. Later, I came to know a somewhat young, black male caseworker of similar qualities. He took the impersonating an intellectual yet a step further. In addition to the pipe he wore a Sherlock-like raincoat and the Sherlock-styled cap. He, however, may have actually worked, I know not either way.

In addition to these characters, there were a few who had stories surrounding them of a more salacious nature, but I will not bore you with these as they are the nature of so much government work. Yet I should tell you that the location of the building was such that at 3:00 p.m. like clockwork the ladies of the night would appear directly in front of our office as we were in the so-called red-light district. They may also have been clients; I have no idea.

CHAPTER FOUR

GREENER PASTURES

Thank God. I moved out of that nasty downtown office to an office often referred to as the "Country Club." No more Ambush Perfume in the elevator every morning. Clean bath rooms with toilet paper. Isn't this great. Just lots of elderly people on Medicaid and food stamps. Lots of working poor on food stamps. But, a caveat, the need to deal with the "if I was black, I'd get something" group. Remember this was some years ago and often enough said, but even twenty-five years ago this was just too laughable as too many suburban whites (and blacks) were also getting food stamps. Today with Obama's removal of the resource (asset) limit for food stamps, my cohorts who are still employed say everyone who applies for food stamps gets them. Not too difficult to believe with the huge increase in recipients.

But presently, as in the past, many non-recipients have the impression that when on food stamps you get enough to feed yourself or your family for the month, this is most generally not true. In fact often the elderly, who often have very low and or subsidized housing costs, even with very low incomes may receive only ten ($10) to twenty ($20) dollars a month in food stamps. Which also shows you they really need it when they continue to reapply (generally yearly). I may have said that people, especially kids, are not starving in the US except in the most extreme of cases. I stand by that with the caveat that they very probably are not eating the best quality and for sure not their preferences.

Let me share some of my experiences at that office with you. The office was small with a dozen or so caseworkers. Thus, pretty much all that happened of interest was seen and heard by many, as at that time we had no cubicles for client or worker privacy. A phone call came through on the receptionist phone line. It was assumed the call was in Spanish. As our Spanish-speaking workers at that office did not receive the additional 5 percent pay for bilingual workers they refused to use Spanish. Hence the then Coordinator (office head) attempted to talk to the client, no good, he then passed the phone to me, a little better, but then a client got involved and it was discovered that the problem was the lady on the phone was Spanish speaking with a severe speech impediment that was still not possible to understand. She was advised to have a friend or relative call for her. Life can be complicated when you have your own personal setbacks. We were feeling a bit miffed by our seeming lack of skills, but it must be said all was done to settle the problem.

Let me tell you about the Russian-born eighty-plus-year-old lady, who was on a program unique to some states to give more elderly and disabled Medicaid benefits called Spenddown. This was essentially a deductible that was needed to be met to become eligible for coverage for the rest of the month. This was a Medicaid expansion option available only in a few states. Well, Mrs. Lenin would come in every month with her son to explain for her, all though her English was very good. Every month it was trials and tribulations. She would present medical receipts previously used or with the dates changed or even grocery receipts; all in hopes that the worker would just accept them and release her medical card.

This sometimes worked, and other times it did not. Then a flurry of drama would occur about the uncaring government who only helped Blacks and etc., and has forgotten Russia was an ally in WWII. I had the unique experience of doing her annual reevaluation for benefits. She sat at my desk and at high speed told me all the issues she had now and previously. I gave her a few minutes, then said, let's start at the beginning. She responded, I was born in Russia in 1892…to which I said a little more recently please, we both had a laugh at her interpretation. For some reason after that interview, the problems with Mrs. Lenin ended.

I, of course, cannot forget mention of the cat-piss lady. The woman was obviously living in a house, apartment, or under a bridge accompanied by a huge troop of undisciplined kitties. During the course of the twenty minute interview, I had to leave my desk repeatedly to breath. She completely reeked, the cats must have been spraying on her clothes. She obviously was in a rather pitiful situation, that she wanted no help in changing. She got her food stamps and never returned. My coworkers, of course, got a really good laugh as I got this assignment.

Not to be excluded, as she was a frequent visitor and cause for comment, was Miss Fox Fur. Miss Fox Fur tended to have a duplicity of personality, i.e., bipolar or similar. She would come in for an interview and talk of how she was so poor she was eating crackers and cat food, please note her coat probably cost more than any other clients or employees. This is not to say she was lying, as she may have been doing this to punish herself for her sins, imagined or otherwise, as a pastor who was aware of her confirmed this to be sometimes true. She also was a problem at mass on occasion as she would run up and prostrate herself in front of the altar, this being very disruptive. The pastor was as anxious as we were for her to seek care, but for some this never happens due to their civil rights, which are such a detriment to them and the balance of their families and society.

You may concur that I am not a card-carrying ACLU member. In fact a large parcel of letters from a local newspaper were delivered to me, with a plea to get her help. The more entertaining side of Miss Fox Fur was when she would lounge at a male workers desk and act lusciously. She would also tell stories of her brother who allegedly was trying to have her thrown in jail for walking the streets and plying her wares. She protested this effusively, yelling I am not a whore, I am a virgin. We would calm her down, letting her know we were not conspiring with the brother to put her in jail. Also note, rather than eat the canned cat food, it was suggested she try the canned tuna, which would be covered by her food stamps along with a side of mac and cheese, both being very inexpensive, sometimes less than the cat food. Although she did get into a lot of high drama she did have a very legit problem, which I believe was finally addressed or she moved on.

Not to be forgotten is Miss Red Head to Foot. Even though I had read of Hirsutism, I was ill prepared for this. Her pastor called as there was no phone and no car, requesting a home visit for her as she was pregnant, note this was allowed but a rare event. So I arrived at the house and was greeted by an average looking young man. He apologized at length as they had not yet unpacked, note they were already there for two months and cardboard boxes were everywhere. No windows were opened, unusual as it was 80 degrees plus with no air conditioning, and all was semi-dark. Flies buzzed all over and their interest in the highly stacked food dishes surrounding Miss Red Head to Foot was ignored. Cleanliness did not appear to be of any propriety as her feet were black with crusted dirt past her ankles, in evidence as she was barefooted.

One would think I would be most amazed with her orangy-red hair from hair to toes and fingers. Including a sparse beard and large quantity of hair (or would fur be more accurate) spilling forth from the top of her v necked dress. Normally, in a less than clean house, I would choose a wooden chair to sit on, but here I would not sit at all. It was obvious there might be some emotional or mental problems also, plus extreme laziness, she would not even reach for a pen, her man would have to intervene to deliver all papers, verifications, and pens. In the course of the interview it was discovered that Miss Red Head to Foot, was not only pregnant, but attempting to seek renewed custody of another child (no I would not be suggesting this). Now to the issue that truly blew my mind was the fact that she not only had this young man waiting on her, but he was not the professed father of the child, further there was yet a different father to the child in foster care. Oh, did I forget to mention that she approached or exceeded 250 pounds. Here I was a recently divorced woman, of I thought average or better looks, and at the time, close to average weight, unable to find a man. I concluded the application/interview as quickly as possible, advising her man that further steps were to be completed in the office, including the need for welfare photo IDs. They protested the lack of a car, I advised of the close to their door bus stop and the ability for him to walk the less than mile to the office. I did not expect she would or could do so. I left, jumped in my car to pull away, with him running up to my window with my pen. I motioned for him to keep it, left unsaid was that Miss Red Head to Foot had obviously not washed her hands in a long time. Sorry, this exceeded my empathy bounds. It was more in the realm of—if you think you have seen everything, wait a second for what comes next.

If you think I am being cruel about this remembered I minimized the situation and made a Protective Service Referral to make sure she got prenatal services and hopefully was closely watched after delivery. But if we did not laugh at some bizarre situations, we would self-implode. Also there is known to be a rather remote area in China where hirsutism is not uncommon, it is said this is the source of some Yeti yore.

I will bore you with only one remaining phenomena (at that office.) That being the incident of the werewolf man. One day at lunch time, by a fluke, the only employees there were a clerical person and myself. At that time there was one unarmed, albeit large and powerful, security officer who also tended not to be present when needed. In rushed someone(thing), who was spraying spittle effusively and moreover, appeared to be foaming at the mouth. I was called to the front desk to deal with a roaring case of lycanthropy. The clerk kept backing up as he spoke which made good sense as his visage was sufficiently scary, even without his hyper-activity and foaming spittle. Now, as you have already read

I did have opportunity to make acquaintance with the hirsute young woman, so I was no stranger to furry people. Further when put into a strange or dangerous situation I, stupidly, based on bravado and curiosity, rather than bravery, tend to let the situation play itself out.

But let me first describe Mr. Lobo better. He had gray-brown fur on the back of his hands and fingers with a beard that continued down his neck, up his cheekbones, and into his ears, which were pointed. His hair was rather long. His nails were yellow-brown and talon-like. His eyes were yellow/brown hazel, with very bushy eyebrows. His hairline came down unusually close to his eyebrows. As it was my job to help people, whatever their genealogy, I did try to assist him. He wanted to go here not there. But had been there without finding here, but why not there. To go there and not here while getting there was imperative. After the rather lengthy version of who's on first lycanthropy style, I sent him on down the road to the Social Security Office, as he seemed to be eligible if not already receiving.

This seemed to please him, although he felt it might not be here or there. The clerk recovered quickly after he left and, of course, the security guard came in shortly after he left. I had never read the riot act so strongly to security before. He of course acted like we were nuts or setting him up to look stupid, if he believed us. This is cold, hard, facts. Sorry for Mr. Lobo as I am sure his social life is limited. Put simply, lycanthropy is real. Should you meet your wolfman in your lifetime I do hope you are not alone and in a safe space. I do hope yours is more fictional, unlike my very real Wolfman.

Let me digress to a situation that came up soon after moving to this office location. At that point I had a boss that was not hateful, but less than agreeable. Maybe because I was new there or because she thought I could do it, she asked me to do a home visit for a husband and wife, who were mentally ill. The man was too manic to come into the office and could not be interviewed unless his mother was there for safety reasons, as he was suspected to have killed his first wife. So apparently I was to be the sacrificial lamb. I went to the apartment and knocked expecting the mother to answer, but no, the man answered with his face being inches from mine. I told him I would wait until his mother came, but his wife was there and more amiable, although also mentally ill. So I did rapidly conduct the interview not telling the results, advising I would mail the outcome. During the entire time he paced rapidly and often came very close and hovered. I let him know to please back up so I could be more comfortable. I finished and returned to the office, letting my then boss know that only phone interviews or office interviews with mother should occur in future. Within a few months his present wife was found dead. He of course was a suspect. Work was seldom boring.

Fortunately, this boss voluntarily left the agency for her own good reasons and a new gentleman began who was very knowledgeable, kinder, but also much more fun. He was well loved by many and became a friend. He was very laissez-faire and that worked so well. We kept in touch and worked together regardless of what office I was at. He died young and was mourned by many.

During his tenure we had a few adults, usually in their fifties or so, who were on General Assistance and required to work some hours for the county each week. General Assistance was a benefit unique to only a few states and in fact is no longer available in any. A few were waiting for approval of disability, but just short of the requirements. They were generally very agreeable and some were with us doing a small amount of cleaning for a few years. A few had problems that were more obviously mental. One notably was the nun, or so she thought. She would show up in various stages of sisterly apparel and leave various prayers on some desks. She also would leave warnings of hell and damnation where she felt they were warranted. She would frequently give short speeches on the inappropriate uses of a person of the cloth in cleaning offices where the morally unclean were present. On more upbeat emotional days she would leave presents of crocheted bookmarks in the form of crucifixes. By the time we became totally used to her presence in the office she just never returned with no explanation that anyone knew about. Unusual became our usual so we missed our characters. We had a few more ladies who were on General Assistance working at our office also cleaning. They also knitted, in fact one was kind enough to knit our boss a penis sheath for the cold weather, how thoughtful. We jumped on helping these ladies to get disability approval as they were under educated and in need, they also were very sweet.

Another interesting situation was the adult client with turrets syndrome. She came with her parents, who were very apologetic, but had little or no control of what was said. The poor caseworker assigned to her interview happened to be black and one of the most sweet, kind, and religious persons I knew at that point in my life. Unfortunately, one of the client's random words she spewed was the n word, mixed with much profanity. I called the caseworker into my office and quickly explained what I assumed was the clients problem and told her I would do the case. Now, she was willing, particularly knowing the situation, but I didn't want her to have to do so. It was great to see someone not hung up on race relations. I was happy to later go to her second-late-in-life wedding. It was great to see someone so really happy to be married, like a real life "Love Story." She was truly a sweetheart.

Another, truly touching situation, was our first AIDS client. This was when people were afraid to use the same pen and breathe the same air as AIDS patients, when there was really no effective treatment and patients died in a few months. I saw the client, but on the floor at an unused desk, rather than in my office (as I was by then a supervisor). I wanted the other employees see me shake hands and treat the client like any other, i.e., with respect and dignity. After that no one questioned interviewing a

HIV or AIDS client. Note, in regards to privacy, we would have to know rather quickly their medical condition, as it allowed for possible expedited Medicaid approval. Quickly, workers went from fear to great empathy, as in the beginning one could almost know someone's diagnosis without being told, due to their great pallor and obvious weight loss, similar to those with advanced cancer. Soon enough employees would know a friend, a cousin, a brother, etc. with a stage of the disease that made them want to help not avoid the client. In the beginning of the AIDS crisis there were frequent new cases, most living only a short time. I got where I could guess an AIDs diagnosis regularly as the client looked similar to some cancer patients, but less healthy. In just three or four years this greatly changed. The clients remained healthy looking much longer, and in fact lived much longer. Fortunately, great progress continues medically and in number of cases.

Lest you think we were uncaring let me tell a few other touchy-feely stories. Most people don't know this but, in special situations, it may be possible to get approval for unusual items that may improve clients lives. I was sent on a home visit for a young man of perhaps thirty years old who lived with his mother. He had severe scoliosis of the spine to the point he generally could not get out of bed, but only roll from one point to the other. As he sat his face was forward and his feet were pointed behind him, so severely was his spine turned. We talked and he was in surprisingly good spirits, but only wished he could get a water bed to help with possible bed sores. I was able to get an override from the state and he and his mother were so grateful. He did have one outlet, a group of motorcyclists would from time to time show up with a sidecar and take him riding. It's great that some people do truly care for others.

Another less dramatic example of special circumstances was a young boy of maybe ten or twelve years old who due to an accident would be in a wheelchair for life. He came in and wanted bicycle tires on his wheelchairs so he could go faster and do wheelies. Well, we hooked him up with a bike store that was willing to accept vouchers and got an override to set him up to do wheelies.

Sometimes things were a little closer to home, so I would have some insight into the problem and could intervene. Once a guy from the neighborhood I grew up in came into the office with no appointment and became argumentative. My family had been friends with all the men in the family, the parents were long ago passed away. I recognized the voice and stepped in as the guard was calling the police as he was refusing to leave. So I talked to him, finding that he felt his sister was refusing to give him his money. He was on disability, probably PTSD from Viet Nam. I called his sister and talked him down, as she handled his money, appropriately so, as he wasn't able to. He left calm and happy.

Another time a disabled brother of my brother's ex showed up at the end of the day in obvious need of medical attention. He literally had foam and blood dripping from an ear, from infection. As I immediately recognized him, I intervened. He told me he was hungry and had no food. I was incensed as I knew he received an inheritance from a father who was a millionaire when that was real money. I took him to a hunger center for bags of food, gave him a twenty, dropped him at his apartment. As soon as I got home I called his sister and let her know he needed to have his family look in on him etc. They didn't call our office a neighborhood service center for nothing.

One further client who would be the epitome of the need for food stamp reform arrived in our office freshly from out of state in what, even forty years ago, would have been a near hundred thousand dollars mobile home. He was promptly seen and denied based on assets and became loudly furious saying - what do you mean I'm not eligible, everyone in Tennessee is on food stamps. I do believe he honestly believed what he was saying, although I'm pretty sure most of Tennessee didn't have his assets. I'm sure some of you still think everyone's on food stamps when you are in line at the supermarket and those in front of you always seem to be. Worse it seems they are the ones with the crab legs and steaks, but more commonly most who receive are either low income, elderly or employed, but low income families.

Now, I would like to introduce a few fellow employees who stood out for various reasons. One later endearing, but initially hostile, persons was a middle aged black women Mrs. Dee, who was not, at first, happy with her move to our "White" office. She sat at the desk next to mine in an open office. Next to her was the Coordinator's secretary, Mrs. Bee. She was a neighbor/friend of mine from my childhood neighborhood. Probably because of age Mrs. Bee and Mrs. Dee got along fine. However, Mrs. Dee always made little digs implying I was "too White" and comments about coming from a "horsey set" exurbia. Which I did, but at the time we had two horses and no saddles as the choice was horse and saddle or two horses no saddles. We became used to riding bareback and didn't want the saddle when given one. More importantly when we lived there it wasn't pricey at all, just a long commute for my father. Pricey came ten years or more after we moved, but at the time it was the best school district in the state.

So, what broke down the barriers was one afternoon when Mrs. Bee was talking about when her father died and they were for a time on welfare, when you couldn't even have a TV set and how they played hide the TV when the worker came for a home visit. I spoke up and said that I was born in the city projects. Mrs. Dee stood up and said "no you weren't," to which I retorted, well yes I actually was. Then I explained how that happened to be and was only until my father married my mother, who was widowed with two children at a time there were few safety nets, so she lived in public housing. They were married shortly after he returned from WWII, when there was a shortage of housing, so we remained in the projects until a house was found.

Mrs. Bee said yes this was real, after this Mrs. Dee warmed up. In fact she was a riot. Once I was interviewing a good looking male client and Both Bee and Dee phoned me during the interview. They wanted to know if I had noticed the size of the bulge in his pants, as I happen to blush easily, I had to excuse myself and walk over to the water cooler, keep in mind these "ladies" were twenty years my senior with children and grandchildren, After I finished with the client, to clarify I asked them did they always do this and they were like - you're kidding, you don't. Well, they proceeded to make fun of me, because he was apparently very well hung and I didn't notice. This became even more convoluted as they watched when he came back again as his case was pended. Then he came back again just to ask a few questions. It provided great entertainment for them.

Mrs. Dee was kind enough when I got a divorce to make sure I was happy. She let me know she could connect me with very young men for $ that could make me very happy and relieve my sexual tensions. I of course thought she was kidding, but no, she knew I didn't want involvement, nor did she, and was using this service also. What a forward-thinking woman, unfortunately I was too prim and proper to avail myself of this service. We became good friends and confidants, even when I moved yet again to another office. Her husband was in many ways a great guy and the love of her life, but got involved with drugs. Things went downhill for them and he became ill and died from a drug-related illness. I of course went to the funeral, the first I attended that was in a store front type church. Unfortunately, Mrs. Dee also became ill maybe a year later, we visited her in the hospital and realized it wouldn't be long. Another funeral to go to, at least many DHS workers had enough sense of comradery to support each other in the important ways.

But, let me tell you a more happy ending story. Ms. Leela moved to our office. She was a delightful slightly older black women who was a widow with children. She was a church going lady and very good with clients. She was admired by most if not all other employees. We were so happy for her when she found a good man who proposed to her. She just glowed for months as she prepared for a traditional white gown church wedding with a lovely reception. I was fortunate to be invited, it was lovely. I believe she retired afterward and she was old enough to do so and had worked long and hard enough.

During my time at this office, President Reagan supported a SSA move to review the status of those on disability, giving them time to present updated medical proof or have benefits suspended or closed until new proof was given. This caused great public outcry. Our agency was contacted by the Bill Moyer's Show to have a client affected by this change to have an unscripted interview by a caseworker. I was asked to do the interview, that should have reflected how negatively this affected people who were disabled. A family not previously on food stamps was found who wanted to have their interview televised to highlight the financial effect on their family.

We expected this to be like a local TV interview with a camera and a spokesperson. But, it was not. There was lights, camera, director, battery packs on me and it turned into a side show. They actually filmed for more than thirty minutes. A coworker who was miffed by my being chosen said it probably would be cut to thirty seconds or never be run. This couple still had income as the wife was laid off from an auto maker. The question should have been why did they have no savings. Well, they did get some food stamps, they were surprised to find they would not be enough to feed them for a month, but were actually intended for three months or so. It's a surprise to everyone, it seems, that food stamps are only a supplement, that where there is income one is to use some to feed your family. They also wanted a referral to a local hunger center for bags of groceries and toiletries, usually we don't get many requests for such from clients with short turn loss and with income still in the home. But, I did so, and they did get help there. Of course the disability was eventually restored as the man was disabled. This was most often the case, but not always. In my opinion, disability did need to be reviewed from time to time, depending on type.

So, in essence Reagan was correct, but often criticized for this action. But, to my credit the filming ran for five minutes in prime time and reran again at a later date. Unfortunately, Hollywood did not call, to my disappoint, as the director and camera man said I was very photogenic and carried the interview very well. But, at least a friend from the training department would forever after refer to my TV career when there were new employees present . It also made me a favorite of the training department and was often called on to train on larger projects. Sadly he was killed in a serious car accident at a young age, and missed by many.

It was not long after this that the final shoe dropped for a supervisor at our office. It appears that a caseworker took exception to him physically throwing one volume of the manual at him. As the supervisor also refused to sign off on so many cases that they encircled his office to a height of perhaps two to three feet as they did not have a signed form that was at that point obsolete, a deal was made. He was sent to another office that needed a supervisor. I was promoted to fill the vacancy. At this point I had been with the agency exactly five years, the minimum at that time to be a supervisor.

My boss was both very smart and very laissez-faire and generally well liked. This was how I worked best. Some thought we didn't work hard enough at that office. Actually we worked smart not hard. As an example a new and unreasonable change occurred. It was called monthly reporting. So every client who had earned income was required to fill out a form and send it along with the representative pay stubs for the month within a few days after the end of the month. We would have to make food stamp budget changes, and send a change letter before the next data processes change date. Our office had many working people, in fact about one thousand cases. It was also perhaps the smallest office in terms of personnel. So we had to process one thousand changes per month in about a ten day window along with our regular changes and reevaluations. We always managed to do so, as we created a process that worked. There were other offices with as few as sixteen working income cases, yet they seldom met their deadlines.

It was rumored that often a token few employees could be found a few doors down at a neighborhood bar. There was some truth to this, mainly close to days end. Did it affect our efficiency, I would say no, with the exception of perhaps one employee, who at some future point in time lost his job for even more disturbing reasons. I must admit on a very few occasions I also could be found there downing a diet coke.

At this office I did a lot of training for the entire office at my bosses request even though he came from the training department. I generally liked doing this so it was a good fit. Sometimes as many of us were friends, with a tendency to find humor in pretty much everything, this did not go smoothly. A case in point would be Miss Figgly's new look. Now Miss Figgly had a bit of a mental problem, which we learned to be very understanding of. She also was very rigid, in application of the rules and very upright in her personal habits. One day I was presenting some new material on the floor rather than in a meeting room, in the midst of the Miss

Figgly came walking in, quite late, so we were all seeing her for the first time that day. Well, I started giggling, then we all fell out. Miss Figgly had recently lost some weight and invested in a new red dress, red lipstick, red shoes, with heels higher than she was able to walk on, ankles bowing out. But the cherry on the cake was the new wig, worn a tilt. I had to take her to the ladies room to set that hairpiece straight in order that we all could stop giggling and proceed.

Another training incident was when a State employee came to present some changes, Mrs. Foostam. Mrs. Foostam as friendly and very agreeable, perhaps to a fault. She was presenting her information to the group when Josh, a caseworker, interrupted asking if she would like to see his baby picture. I intervened and told him she would not like to, as I had seen the baby picture. He interrupted a few more times before stopping. A while later I stepped into the coordinator's office to find Josh in fact showing his very altered baby picture to giggling Mrs. Foostam. The photo was a snapshot of Josh as a toddler with a penis a porn star would be proud to have. Mrs. Foostam handled this very well, although I don't believe she ever returned to that particular office.

CHAPTER FIVE

PASS GO, DO NOT COLLECT $200

As often occurs when there was a new director, there was a big employee shuffle, as in the words of the new director, let's call him Mr. Latino, he wanted the faces in the office to look like "salt and pepper." As you might believe this manner of speaking was not well received by many. But worse, at great inconvenience to many of the supervisors, workers, and most coordinators we were shifted to new locations. I referred to this as busing, after the style of student busing during the school integration era.

Let me show a few areas where he was so very out of touch with reality. The state made a move to drop a program that was not federal and only a very few other states even had. It was called General Assistance and was cash payment, very minimal, and medical coverage for single men and women with no income. Mr.

Latino was obsessed with the negative impact this would have on this population and expected a huge increase in homelessness. As he knew little of reality about public assistance he did not know that many of the General Assistance population were already homeless. There was a movement to have all losing benefits to ask for hearings, which, of course, they lost. But few requests were received. Mr. Latino would always ask where these people had gone. Homelessness did not increase. The soup kitchens were not deluged. He just could not accept they probably were back home with mama, or had always lived there, or lived with the current girlfriend. More importantly, they may have used this minimal income as an explanation to police as to where their support came from.

Another huge conundrum to Mr. Latino was the fact that many children on assistance did not have regular doctor checkups nor have the necessary vaccinations required until they were refused school admission. He insisted that the clients did not know they could use their medical cards to get these benefits. Also he believed most doctors would not accept them. It is true that some doctors would not accept them, but the numbers were and are grossly exaggerated and many clients went to a clinic, where they were received. So Mr. Latino set up a medical station in the front lobby of the main welfare office to give on-the-spot vaccinations. Most clients who did not yet have their kid's shots were not interested, did not have time for them, or otherwise refused. Close to zero clients made use of the clinic. He was so disappointed, and just couldn't understand why this was not a success. He could not face that some mothers do not put their children first. In fact later there was a move to pass a state law requiring children to have timely vaccines to receive cash benefits. This did not fly, apparently the adult client's rights again superseded the children's. Another liberal director became disenchanted and subsequently left, unknown if by invitation or of his own volition.

Let me tell you of the lovely surroundings at this new office. Note this is new as in different, not newly built. In fact the building had historical significance which was not obvious on the floor we occupied. The only historical element on our floor was a history of gigantic roaches. They were often a topic of discussion, When I asked the building manager about them I was frequently told that they sprayed for them, but I should consider myself lucky that they were or were not German roaches. This meant they did not reproduce quickly.

When I moved to this office, I was left an object d'art. That meaning the previous supervisor had kindly left me his mounted—think squirrels or deer heads—roach. The new coordinator was retiring and using up six months of sick time, for which she would have been paid 25 percent of normal pay if she retired with it outstanding. She was mean as the Wicked Witch of the West, or is that East? She blamed all that she had contact with that she had been moved to this new location for the balance of her career. She only came to work one day per week in order not to need to provide a doctor's excuse. She kept her door closed at all times. I, by way of a posted note, was assigned the office of someone I found very offensive in a male domineering and marginal grooming manner. The type that always reclined back in their swivel chairs with their legs widely separated, like Putin, but generally powerless. Excuse me, but he just didn't have the stones to pull this off.

So I sat down in this chair and promptly was almost ejected as in a "Bond" movie. He had so broken down this chair to be both unusable and a risk to limb and life. In the meantime I received a phone call from my previous boss to see how things were going and I filled him in on the ugly details. He let me know the other office had been washed down including inside desks etc., with disinfectant by the gentleman who left me his mounted cockroach solely and specifically for my use. That was the office I wanted originally, but was denied by wicked witch. So I marched into her office and let her know I was moving into that space and as she planned not to be there for most of six months she needed not to hassle me as someone needed to know what to do, and further, I would let it be known she had set me up for injury (chair). I walked out and believe I never had reason to speak to her again in her remaining time there, nor did anyone else.

Now let us discuss the roach population further. These were not the roaches some city dwellers know. They did not come out at night and scatter when the lights came on. These were large enough and self-assured enough that they came out in the naked light of day with the office full of clients and employees and slowly, but steadily marched across the floor, or desk, or lunch room tables.

So assured were they that they were known to fly down from the false ceiling during my lunch and light on my shoulder, followed by a great and unseemly outburst, so I was told. But I let it be known that the presence of fearless and immense roaches fighting me for my well-earned lunch was what was unarguably unseemly.

A further incident was when a very reserved fortyish male caseworker, who was always in suit, white shirt, and tie was physically violated by a roach of good size that crawled up his pant leg during a client interview. This gentleman was a Latino, which is not what prompted him to jump up and do the La Cucaracha Dance. But, dance though he may, shaking his leg rather violently, the roach would not leave the comfort of, perhaps, his tightywhities. Finally, he ran to the men's room and evicted the roach from the warmth and comfort of his body. He and his client were notably upset, but to no avail, as the management might spray, and control rather than destroy the population. Remember in your own home and business always call an exterminator, not a pest control company, as by definition it will be a losing proposition.

Now, one would think this would be the end of the roach events, but the most raucous of all was the day when a very large,

ALBINO roach, pink eyes and all, went running across the main floor of the interview area. Workers were screaming, clients were up on chairs, some of us were laughing, it was a three-ring circus. Someone went to kill the roach, to which I yelled, "Nooooo! Save it for the zoo!" Unfortunately it escaped to create havoc elsewhere. I dreamed of a brass plaque at the zoo with "Donated by County Welfare Employees" under the display. Again a lost step towards notoriety. Life is not fair.

So, in the true manor of a caseworker, investigator, welfare cop, mentally I began documenting DOA, date of death, for the various roaches. As the building management was allegedly to have the floors swept, washed, or vacuumed daily there should have been no dead roaches left in place for days on end. Therefore, to prove our point, and be the true leader I was, I began leaving post it notes on the dead roaches, i.e., Date of death 010195; 010595 not yet buried or disposed of. After the building manager, who was about eighty years old and resembled the 1950s department store floor walker, very Dickens, was apprised of my roach accounting system, he became very angry. I advised the resolution was to get the cleaning crew to clean and the pest company to do their thing. Be angry with them not me. Well, this led to a distinct reduction in the roach activity and increase in cleanliness. The building manager never forgave me for making him follow the lease requirements.

CHAPTER FIVE, SCENE TWO

LET US ENTERTAIN YOU

As time went on the never-present coordinator of the office retired after using six months or so of sick time. Most people who read this will look at the public servant not doing their job rather than the supervisors doing her job also because that is what occurs. Often the least important level is the top. Now we must discuss the most novel of bosses I ever experienced.

This gentleman? Mr. Deletante, was the most flamboyant of gay men, although, to my knowledge, not a cross-dresser. He also was at war with the balance of power for transferring him to that office to fill the opening. He behaved badly to retaliate. We became the laughing stock of the agency while continuing to do our jobs in spite of the circumstances.

At first I enjoyed the entertainment after the previous sour-faced, never present twit, as did others. After all, few of us were used to the coordinators who either know or do much, there were, of course, exceptions. As time went on this did change a bit.

It was rapidly obvious that Mr. Deletante was infatuated with another gay man, Mr. Coolbeans. Mr. Coolbeans was in a long term monogamous relationship and really wanted to be left alone. Mr. Deletante simply would not leave him alone and I was often called upon to be a de facto chaperone. Mr. Coolbeans came up with the idea of getting something to keep Mr. Deletante occupied so that we both could more easily do our jobs. He suggested we walk down the street and purchase a parakeet and cage, so he may have a pet to occupy his time, as he had mentioned how he liked them. So we did so. We walked down picked out a chatty parakeet and presented…? Him? To Mr. Deletante.

He was overcome by what he thought was our thoughtfulness and generosity. This was followed by too few days of calm and ability to do our actual jobs.

Soon Mr. Deletante called us in to announce that his parakeet needed a mate, a gay male as he had determined that it was a boy/ How escapes me. I was tasked with going with him to pick a mate. This involved getting every one, employees and customers, in the store into the selection process. Mr. Deletante let all know that a male was needed so that they could be soul mates and lovers. Please know I did this on my lunch hour as I did take my job seriously. So a parakeet was purchased.

This worked as entertainment for our boss for perhaps a week or two until he began letting them out of the cage in his rather expansive office. This accelerated to the point the birds escaped his office during working hours. Not one to control his exhibitionism, he paraded around the office with clients in place, probably drunk as a skunk. He proceeded to dive under desks to retrieve his birds. Workers came to me to deal with the problem. I came forward snatched a bird out of his hands and marched him to his office, closing the door behind us. I let him know via words and hands on bird that if the birds were out of the cage again I would break their f—-ing necks.

Soon after this another problem arose. Mr. Coolbeans became very ill and was hospitalized. Mr. Deletante was incensed when he found this out and wanted to call and visit at the hospital. I was in contact as possible with Mr. Coolbeans, as we had become friends, and he clearly wanted no contact with Mr. Deletante. He became progressively more ill and I was updated by his partner. It was not long before he succumbed to his illness. We were all saddened by this news.

Worse, Mr. Deletante went off the deep end. He quickly found an outlet for his immediate needs, bringing this much younger bar foundling into the office; for what reason escapes me. He let me know that he took him home that night and scrubbed him several times with a scrub brush as he reeked of the streets and had lice. This escapade lasted perhaps two weeks or so with the friend showing up with him at the office occasionally. This was a relief to all, particularly myself, as he left us to our work. I also told him to take the birds home along with his new friend. He did listen to this, but only after one additional incident with his friend. The next day before they came up to the office he beat his friend up in the building lobby. Goodbye friend at least at work.

Things were going progressively downhill. It was getting more and more difficult to take care of the clients' needs and employees' questions and complaints regarding the non-leadership. At perhaps this point I had a phone call from an assistant director. Did the coordinator have a TV in his office? Is it true he had birds in his office? I was not aware, but at his previous location he was ordered to remove his TV, to my knowledge he had none at this office, unless he did a great job of hiding it. As to the birds, I let the assistant director know that yes, he had had birds, but had taken them home at my request. Further, Mr. Coolbeans and I bought them for him to keep him entertained. I was told they couldn't believe this as I had a great reputation for doing my job and seeing that others did so also.

Well, it was said that Mr. Deletante was also to be doing his job. I explained that this is probably never going to happen. The best to be expected was that we should be free to do our work. At this point I was also doing the job of two other supervisors, so it was said the one position would be filled and the assistant director would stop in more often. I also starting getting regular phone calls from my previous boss to see if I was OK and how out of control Mr. Deletante might be. Things were crazy, but the job was getting done in spite of him. You do understand that this man had a good many years with the county and perhaps much protection as he didn't start these behaviors yesterday and could be a lot of fun and be very agreeable. The real problem was he should have been a companion not a boss. Things had to get so very bad before I could say enough. I must be in charge of whistle-blowing on top of everything else.

To further demonstrate that his shenanigans were well known at the agency, let me share another experience. Mr. Deletante and I, as we did enjoy each other's company, went to lunch one day at a well-known restaurant within a department store that sadly no longer exists. We were standing waiting for the elevator when his attention was diverted by a, assuredly fake, marble statue of David. He, of course, began fondling its genitalia, then the elevator doors opened and his highly placed female friends stepped out, giving me a frown, as much to say that I am enabling and leading him astray. Just another day.

As to enabling I must confess to another incident. I had a light-skinned black woman in my unit. She came with a history of dabbling in voodoo. Shall we call her Madame Marie LeBeaux. Rumor was that her previous supervisor had been intimidated by her and kept a broom in her office to prevent any hex being successful. Why a broom? This I do not know. I thought this was hilarious, certainly not a cause for concern. However, as time went on I was beginning to also feel uncomfortable around her. So I felt a preemptive strike was in order. I took Mr. Deletante with me to a nearby meat market to get some chicken feet. I took these chicken feet and looked on her chairback for some of her long black hairs. I took the hairs and wrapped them around the chicken feet and put them in an interoffice envelope. I placed the envelope on her chair for her to find in the morning. I had no further negativity from her. Did I mention I had to get Mr. Deletante to dumpster dive to get the chicken feet?

Next came a call from personnel giving the OK to fill the uncovered supervisor's position. Mr. Dilettante was given the top three names on a list of employees who had taken the then-used state test for supervisors. He was required to pick from those three or find good reason to go further down the list. Well, on that list was a well-known agency character who was either a transvestite or a transsexual. I specify this as it was never documented whether any surgical changes, or for that matter hormonal steps, had been taken. As this dress-sporting individual had an extremely rough, male countenance, some had the view that they were sharing a bathroom with, not a transsexual, but a voyeur. When yet another man in the agency began, out of the blue, to show up for work in dresses, he was given notice that some medical evidence was necessary to change sexes in mid-stream. What a conservative approach. Back to the employment interview in progress—worse he or she, as I came to know of her from sources at her previous site, was plain mean and harsh to clients and staff. I was asked to sit in on the interview and it was plain by the written piece she was to submit that she had very poor writing skills. I did let her and Mr. Deletante know I was aware of her poor interpersonal skills with both coworkers and clients that were akin to meanness.

Well, as it happens, Ms. Lit as in litigation was selected. Mr. Deletante shared with me his wish to create a situation for the employees of the office, who he felt had turned against him, requiring him to be more careful in his behaviors. I got a call from personnel asking why she was selected and I let it be known it was to punish the county and this office's employees and Ms. Lit intended to be very dictatorial to assuage treatment she viewed as personal slights in the past. Thus Mr. Deletante was required to submit, in writing, a hitherto never required step—his reasons for making the decision to promote Ms. Lit. He was incensed, but did so, hence Ms. Lit became a supervisor. I received calls from many at many levels to explain how this had happened, apparently it was becoming more and more obvious that I was the de facto "in charge person" at this office. More stories of Ms. Lit will follow as she was a chapter or so in herself.

Somewhere in all this craziness I received a phone call from the director that I was to attend all meetings that Mr. Deletante would normally attend, whether he did or not. Perhaps I didn't mention to you that the director had called me previously to ask simply, "Is he drinking again?" This I could not answer with certainty as he didn't smell of alcohol, perhaps as he drank vodka and carried it in a briefcase, which he had no other use for as he did no work. I would be expected to attend upper management meetings in order to convey updates in information to other office employees. I would be added to the notification list and should not be concerned that himself would not be happy with this. He was on a slippery slope.

Lest it be believed that public employees could not be fired, let me tell you of steps I found necessary to take. One of the gentlemen(?) that I was unfortunate enough to have in my unit was Mr. Poo Bungler. Poo reeked to high heaven and was known throughout the agency for being odorific. He also was a bungler as he knew not of social conventions. He spoke in rapid-fire, few clients complained even though he generally was behind in his work, particularly case closings. I wouldn't complain about a few extra checks either, further due to his speech problems many didn't know what he may have said. But he was kindly, which in the welfare world gave you a wide berth of acceptance. Generally, regardless of slowness in case approvals or changes, there would be fewer complaints than for the professional and timely workers. Supervisors and above loved professionalism, clients loved it far less.

So as little time passed before my asthmatic lungs had breathed the last breath of Mr. Bungler's effluvium. No, really, he had a sweater that smelled like moldy, wet dog. Further, he wore this sweater often. I am very allergic to mold. I began to wear perfume regularly to get the smell of him out of my nose and lungs. I also received increasing complaints of his odor from fellow employees. Further, I received phone calls making fun of me for having him in my unit. Well, this was the last straw. I began writing him up for appearance and lack of professionalism. I indicated that if at any time a client or a co-worker complained of his odor he would be sent home and his pay docked. He, of course, filed a complaint with the union. There was a hearing. I, of course, won. This also became agency gossip.

Next he came in with dirty shirts. I warned him. He said he had no hot water in his apartment and could not afford to move. I foolishly asked why, to which he said his girlfriend needed a refrigerator, so he bought her one. It should be noted that it filtered down to me via security that he was observed with his "girlfriend" at the county jail "swapping spit" with her. She had been arrested for prostitution. Why could she not use her earnings for her own refrigerator. I advised Mr. Bungler I did not care if he had to go down to the river and pound his laundry on the rocks, he would be clean or sent home. He was sent home and allowed to return being docked for the time, but advised next time he would stay home the whole day and be docked (which would give him little refrigerator money).

Next was the situation where Mr. Bungler came to work without a belt on his pants, but walked around holding his pants up so that they would not fall down. Yes, I fumed, counted to ten, then twenty, thank God we were still able to smoke. Then I acted. I called Mr. Bungler into my office. Asked why he was walking around holding up his pants. He told me his belt was too big, so it wouldn't keep his pants on. I told him to fix his belt or buy a belt or tie on his pants with a rope, but he wasn't walking around holding his pants up under my supervision. Long story, short, I told him to pull his belt off, I punched a new hole in with my old fashioned paper spindle and let him know to get a new one tout de suit.

Next incident was where he actually had a client kneeling on the floor to sign something as he had another client at his desk and was multitasking. Yes, another worker came to me and I did come down hard on this impropriety. He just didn't know, said the client was okay with this. Well, I wasn't. He was made to clean up his desk area and never commit such a faux pas again. In the meantime I was continuing to write up and give formal warnings, he knew he was wrong and after reaching top level of labor negotiations began trying in every way possible to comply. It didn't help that he had been allowed to get away with this forever and that his new soul mate was the office union steward. Also important was that the union steward had his own list of work and social faults, but that will follow.

Inevitably my methods did bear fruit and Mr. Bungler did his very best to comply. So much so that he bought me a gift to thank me for my help. I also received kudos from throughout the agency as he was recognized as an irreparable problem. He became a go-to person when I needed a task done.

As to the union steward, he also had some lesser cleanliness issues, but did have a physical disability that put limits on him. It didn't help that his mother still bought his clothes and that he still lived at home. His shirts had a very much washed and wrinkled appearance and I don't think the ties were ever cleaned. This was a shame as he tended to wear his lunch on them. His mother purchased his clothes in the boys department as he was very thin and they were cheaper there. This was Mr. GI Joe as he would become very excitable when he felt he or someone else was wronged, and would appear to be fighting the issue as he spoke about it.

As he still lived at home and was unable to drive, Mr. GI Joe had few expenses and was known to have sizable savings although he did have one regular expense. He loved to visit the clubs that had "lady" pole dancers and the like. He kept a photo album of himself mud and Jell-O wrestling with the "ladies." He loved to carry these around as he visited several offices as a union rep, and letting anyone who would look at them know one girl was his "girlfriend." He also had a bad habit of getting so excited when he had a marginally pretty, young blonde at his desk that he had trouble controlling his spastic limbs.

Further, all eligibility rules seemed to go out the window. In reviewing a few cases, I asked him where the verifications were and he simply said, but she told me, so I believed her. He had the nerve to get very angry when I questioned his methods, and advised this was no longer acceptable. Others hadn't questioned him as he was disabled and inclined to get too upset. Of course, I must be a prig as the thought of him with these young and pretty girls revolted me, as the gossip always was that he was such a pervert. I guess I was just intolerant and couldn't believe all the mothers who let him touch their kids. Further, he was known to hang out at a park that was meant for young children. As he was not a parent this would put him on most people's pervert radar. A number of coworkers commented on their revulsion in seeing him touch children. He probably hadn't a clue what others thought and was probably innocent in thought and deed, but to prevent problems, I let him know my concerns and warned him what would happen if there was ever a complaint.

Mr. GI. Joe also had some skin problems, with occasional outbreaks of acne like cysts. This was so unacceptable to Mr. Deletante who was so incensed by this lack of attention to his skin that he approached Mr. GI Joe with intent of popping his pimples right on the office floor with other workers and clients present. Just a bit of personal space infringement, would you say. Fortunately Mr. GI Joe put a kibosh to this. He later mentioned it and I discreetly suggested he see a dermatologist as we then had good free health care

Back to Mr. Deletante, he must have been drinking more, which he presumably covered up by bringing in a bottle in a briefcase, a new affectation. He lost his self-control so much that he began bringing in groups of gay friends that were of less than salient backgrounds and remaining in his office with the door closed for hours. The group would include the brother of a well-known local politician. I felt sorry for him as he seemed such an innocent, not so much by age, but perhaps simplicity. He didn't need to be in the circle of Mr. Deletante's friends.

There were also several incidents where he noticed a decent-looking male client sitting at a worker's desk being interviewed. He actually would call the worker to have them bring the client to his office to complete the "interview" after the worker had finished theirs. These were closed-door "interviews." Also note the only other client contact was once when a client phone call was put through to him, when he screamed for all to hear, "How dare you call me! I don't talk to clients!" Then he promptly hung up and proceeded to berate the clerk who had put the call through to him.

Worse, he ordered a birthday cake for an employee at a nearby bakery. He picked the cake up and brought it back to the office. He discovered that there was a one-letter misspelling in the name. He became visibly enraged and grabbing the large cake returned to the bakery. He nearly threw the cake across the counter accompanied by a verbal dressing-down. I received a phone call from police officers called to the scene advising that no charges would be brought as long as he never set foot in the bakery again. No cake that day. He returned to the office and I was besieged with comments indicating his behavior had progressed to the point that employees were fearful. At this point I contacted the associate director who called in security, who removed him. He was off for a short period while given opportunity for rehab.

Shortly after he returned, both he and I were at an offsite meeting, when he was seized by the DT's (delirium tremens), which I had never witnessed before. I cleared the room immediately and called in a security man that I knew would be professional and discreet. I still wanted him to be able to maintain some sense of self-respect. This was an unfortunate result of trying, by himself, to stop a heavy alcohol addiction, and maybe greater problem. After this he did not return to work. I do hope he retained his pension rights as he had some good years. But worse, he passed away only a few years after. This information, among other demeaning facts, were disseminated by no less than the sleaze-bag he had promoted, who used his personal data to follow him within our system. This gross violation I passed on to those who should have acted, but feared Ms. Lit.

So temporarily we had an associate director, maybe once a week or so, popping in their head to see if all is well. Why did no one pop in their heads when all was so crazy. Now that our alleged boss was gone all was fine. But this was perhaps an imposed requirement so that more did not go wrong. This was a period of crazy transitions. The associate director was retiring and the long-time, much-respected director was also planning to retire. I am thanked for all I have done to hold the office together and by one, foolishly trusted and respected, assistant director that he would do his best to see that I was promoted. Well, this didn't happen as he knew there was already a new director, very political—no one else looked at—in the works. The new director saw that a friend, who was then a caseworker, who gave her a ride to work every day, got the promotion. She was not though sent to our office, remember she had to provide that ride to work for director, but instead unseated another coordinator who was angry to say the least by her unsolicited change in venue. What drama.

This new coordinator we will call Ms. PhD as she was working on that in hopes of retiring very soon and teaching at a college level in her post-retirement. Unfortunately, this move to our office made proximity to school a bit of a problem, but doable. So she pouted for a few weeks with her door closed. Well, I did not intend to do her job, as I was done with the mistake of taking on more than I was paid to do, so I knocked on her door and let her know she needed to be open for business. It should be noted that she was competent if initially unwilling. After a time she chilled, I did mention to her that we didn't want her here either so complain to someone who cares.

Ms. PhD and I came to a meeting of the minds in order that the clients be serviced. Also she had just inherited a supervisor from the General Relief Program that had been disbanded. In General Relief her duties encompassed showing up at work sites to see if the worker showed up or not. There was no need to know rules and regulations nor understand supervision. This women was totally incompetent and lazy as the day is long. For clarity we will call her IKAP, an acronym for I Know A Politician. So that you not judge me as unkind, Ms. IKAP publicly stated repeatedly that she knew nothing about the public assistance and had no intention of learning. She also made it very clear that she got her job through a specified politician and we could do nothing about that. Generally speaking she was likeable, but I calculated her salary and benefits over thirty years to be in excess of one million dollars, hence the largest case of personal welfare fraud I personally knew.

Ms. IKAP was liked by caseworkers that wanted a quick signature as she never questioned anything because she wouldn't know where to start. If they actually wanted an answer they came to me. There were other criticisms of her, as she would not handle any personnel issues that involved those who picked up her lunch or did other personal favors. Further she would not know how to handle a personnel problem other than to give it lip service.

A particularly difficult problem that Ms. IKAP refused to acknowledge or address was Mr. Pornophile. Mr. Pornophile was stalking a particularly pretty coworker. He left gifts on her desk daily and sometimes more often. After the first few times she became very upset by this and asked that he not do so any longer. Then she began getting strange packages at home, a few being of the brown wrapper type. When she checked with the senders they all said that they were requested under her own name. She finally reported this problem to the police and the gifts and packages did end. However when this had been reported to Ms. IKAP it fell on deaf ears. Later when the agency changed to computerized caseloads with internet access by caseworkers, Mr. Pornophile was very often seen by others accessing porn sites. This complaint also was ignored. Even when there were general notification warning not to use the internet for personal use, he was not warned about his porn use. But he did do his casework generally properly and also timely, so in that regard was valuable to Ms. IKAP; he also gave her gifts, picked up her lunch, and was generally polite to all. The rest of us thought he was a sleaze and he was somewhat shunned. In fact many held the opinion that he would someday show up on the telly in a really poor light, like a police standoff or such.

I should probably mention to you, in no particular order, my experience with firing people or having them accept demotions. I say this as it is often said that people working in government jobs cannot be fired. On the surface there is truth to this, but for those who truly deserve firing or demotion it is possible for the diligent superior to carry off. In fact I had a reputation for being very adept in this skill. Others were advised on occasion to call me for the how to instructions. The more important reason to write about this is that some of my fires and demotes were particularly skilled at not working, to a degree that was often entertaining. This was true only in retrospect as someone has to do or undo what they have done or failed to do. Some, however, were just plain stupid or minimally out of their league. Done correctly this was high skills work.

Another problem, which I will mention again and often, was that the politically or otherwise connected person was seldom asked if they would be able to do the job they were asking help in getting. More often than not the answer was no. In fact let me tell you about an interview that I sat in on. A gentlemen showed up who was designated as a must interview by human resources. A must interview is a step or so below a must hire. So we interviewed this gentlemen only to find out that he didn't even know what job he was applying for, nor did he want the job, he wanted a job, but this was just too much work. He was, though, ever so polite and very well educated.

Let me tell you of a firing of a young man who had applied for a pay check, but not a job. He was extremely well connected. In fact he let me know, without delay, that he had more than one neighbor who was in State or Federal Government at elective levels, In fact he did neighborly tasks for them. He delivered this information to me in a chatty manner not a threatening manner, at first. His name was Mr. Sports because that was his degree area, which became very obvious. I'm sure his GPA was not reason to brag, even given the major.

Well, Mr. Sports began his second day of work by leaving, after signing in, to get a muscle-man's breakfast. He proceeded to eat this at his desk. I of course let him know that it was not OK to come in, run out to get his breakfast, then eat it at his desk, sometimes with a client at a neighboring desk. The question would be should I have to even have said this? So he cleaned his act up by sneaking a breakfast in the lunch room. Lunch was also treated as an important part of the day. Even when he tried it was obvious he was learning little. But, to give credit, he did dress well for the job. In fact I believe he thought of himself as very quickly upwardly mobile.

I quickly decided this would not work. So, I took a very unusual step and gave him a possible probationary notice much earlier than the traditional date. He was livid. How dare I. Now he had politically connected agency employees visiting at his desk to commiserate, and undoubtedly assure him he would pass probation and be OK. Instead of beginning to develop good work habits, i.e., no long breakfast breaks, etc., he became somewhat openly hostile.

Well, ultimately and quickly I proceeded to fail him early on in his probation period. In other works a quick and clean firing. Mr. Sports further had the nerve to threaten me physically. Did he think I would cave? Underneath his façade he was just a thug in a suit. So, out the door he went.

Yet I was not yet done with him. The phone calls questioning my abilities and whether I was racist began. Anyone in the agency with a bit of sense knew it takes much time to get a replacement employee. If a new hire they would have to go through two months of training, then you would again start internally training them. In the meantime you would need to reassign that case, often completing some cases in progress yourself. There is no benefit to you in firing or demoting an acceptable worker. The last time I was questioned about Mr. Sports and my alleged predilection to racism was six months after he left. At this time I was with the agency about ten years and never before had the question arose. Who would be stupid enough to even ask the question but a soon to become director.

Even more indicative of politics in play was the fact that Mr. Sports soon was working for the city. The city and board of elections was where the agency failures often went when politically connected or those with sympathetic friends.

My oh my. Why do these things happen to me! Yet another less than learned new hire. I say this as Miss Basket gained many of college credits literally learning to weave the proverbial basket, in addition to other less than edifying courses. Miss Basket also had a long history of public assistance herself and received her degree later in life, which is not related to her stupidity, but just part of the reality. She also would need to ultimately find employment elsewhere. As perhaps a parting gift to me, Miss Basket, made formal racism claims to two EOC type of agencies. They kept pursuing this ridiculously even though black, brown, and white in the office all disputed her claims. Yet we had a black woman in the office who often enough used anti-white racist comments, who later was irresponsibly promoted. To her poor whites were inbred, white trash, and crackers. She did tell me in an open way that she could never trust white people. Nobody though, was running around charging her with racism. On another note I once rode in her car, never again. In the middle of winter I had to open the window, although we just rode a few blocks, as the weed spell was so strong I couldn't breathe. Enough of the race discussion as most of us were very open and uncaring what race one was, instead how people interacted with us.

Sorry, but I'm not quite done with the race issue, but in a very complementary way. Recently, many years after my retirement, a few work friends and I were sitting and discussing what we were going to wear to an upcoming event. As we all were now a few years older we did get into a discussion of "Spanks" and other garments. I immediately remembered two black ladies who were very well endowed but kept thing upwards and inwards as things should be. In other words they had impressive and very restrained racks. I suggested finding out where they went to handle these problems as most of us came from the generation that let everything hang out. These were fond memories.

Another black lady I remember very fondly, Mrs. M., for one thing she had recently been promoted from a clerical position to a caseworker before we converted to on line case entry. She came to me often for help, but after a time acknowledged this was too much for her, and voluntarily was demoted rather than be stressed excessively, further she wanted to be able to be proud of a job well done. She opened her heart to me. We had an older white lady, Ms. T as in tight, who was best explained as wrapped too tightly wound and judgmental. One day the three of us were in the lunch room when a discussion came up over spousal abuse and self-defense cases where abuser was killed. Ms. T announced loudly that never justified they could just leave, exiting stage left. At that point Mrs. M and I were soon alone. Mrs. M told me she had never let anyone else know this, but she had killed her husband in self-defense as she thought this time he would surely kill her as the attacks had escalated. She asked what I thought. I surely thought she was a brave woman who did what she had to do for herself and kids, but better not to share with others as many could be stupidly judgmental. I was also proud that she would trust me to share this with me. I was sorry later that she passed away from a major stroke before I was able to visit her.

Ms. T also made another judgmental boomerang. Again in the lunchroom she opined that people shouldn't live together before marrying. To which another commented strongly, "You're a shacker, aren't you?" She obviously walked into that glass houses comment. Which also brings to mind the old adage, if you can't say nothing nice…

Another favorite in the cast of characters who deserves at least an honorable mention is Motorcycle Mama. Her mode of dress was truly not the best, but not actionable. She was a delight, though when recounting her households habits and family dynamics. Her husband was known to repair his Harley in the kitchen. He was very kind to her, though, as due to a wicked winter and not enough money for her own boots, he allowed her to wear his. Her son was on his way to prison for a very long sentence as he, didn't mean to, but did, beat up and murder the mother of his child. He really only meant to give her a good beating. He called Mama at work often, reversing charges, so he could tell her he loved her, and oh, please send money. I think his sentence was life. I'm sure it will be shorter for good behavior, unless he loses his temper, that can happen.

Someone who many found very endearing was a new hire I actually was able to pick myself was Father Charity. He was very well educated, well mannered, and empathetic. He was also a gay man who had left the priesthood, their loss. One more qualities of interest was his extensive vocabulary, which was not abridged. He had an extensive usage of profanity which came out whenever he became frustrated with our bureaucratic complexity. I didn't want to be rigid or too limiting, but did insist he stop using the two C-words. He did later return to the priesthood when gay but celebrant became acceptable. What a great caring person.

Enter another new hire who was not straight out of school, maybe early forties, came to our office, Senorita Desaperens. To be noted, she was married, but had some difficulties remembering this, therefore, Senorita. At this time it was obvious I was the adult in the room, i.e., in charge of the office. Hence much of interest was told to me, work issues, gossip, etc. Some very strange beliefs were associated with her. Further she was a social worker and not able to absorb fully that the two month training program of rules and regulations was given to her for a purpose. She liked to think that the lady at her desk was to be given help based on emotional feelings. In short, she thought she was Evita Peron, part of her rainbow coalition, come to me and I will make everything possible. Yet another element to her story was that more and more she was seeking out a new hire in my unit, Naïve Joe, who was perhaps twenty years her junior, who also had a loose attachment with reality.

Senorita Desaperens stepped out to have a cigarette, my curiosity whetted, I followed. The conversation quickly moved to her obvious interest in Naïve Joe. At first she became somewhat hostile, accusing me in also acting the cougar (only a hint of truth). I clarified that she could be involved with Naïve Joe or anyone else, I was just curious as to the attraction, unless she was just mothering him. Well, she relaxed and went on to tell me they both had long held interests in extraterrestrials.

Senorita Desaperens did admit to an actual encounter with aliens, not of the trump illegal variety. Well, I, of course, found this very entertaining. But, try as I might, I could get no real details on her interaction. Didn't know if she had actually been transported, but maybe, didn't know if she was examined, no sex contact memories, boring, boring, boring. I lost interest. What I had hoped to hear was some experience reminiscent of *South Park*, with erector sets and antennae sticking out of private parts i.e., anal probs. But, again, no, just boring.

However, it did not end here. After a few months passed both Senorita and Naïve Joe did not show for work one day. No phone calls, just no shows. Of course imaginations flowed, money was on them running off together. Next day Senorita's husband shows up unannounced to find out what's happening. Well, we thought he would know. Then an uncle of Naïve Joe, who of course had a relative working in the agency, calls to get the low down. Well, as he was much concerned, I did relent and let him know a kinder version of the ongoing gossip. Eventually reality came to light, which alas mirrored our imaginations. They had simply run off together like young lovebirds, well one was young. This flight was without the assistance of extraterrestrials. Damn, again we would need to wait months for a new hire.

I must digress. All this extraterrestrials talk, or should we just say ETs, reminds me of a much earlier client I once interviewed, He was young and truly troubled. He didn't so much want to apply for benefits of any kind, but instead wanted to check to see if "the government" was following his every movement. He wanted to know this without offering any data to check anything, because if he gave his info, then of course we could track him. I let him know that this office was not tracking him, although I couldn't speak for other government agencies. He also was concerned that the tracking was being done by non-Earth agencies or entities. He knew that somehow tracking devices had been put in his body and could feel the hum and vibration often. Sometimes he wore a hat made of tin foil in an effort to receive and decode the messages. I couldn't help, but he was relieved that our office was not tracing his movements, one less worry. I looked at him and visualized the tin man from "Oz."

Lest you think we never went the extra mile, let me tell you of a very touching and frustrating situation. This client was brought directly to my attention as it was obvious that she needed some help but, also an intervention of some type. She was older, but not yet old enough for Social Security based on age. After finding out that she claimed to be three years pregnant after being raped by her landlord. I knew this was a disability case, however she was seeing no doctors or counselors. She had been sent to Social Security in the past, but was never even given an appointment for an interview as when she was asked if she was claiming disability, she would say no, I'm just pregnant. Anyone who talked to her for a minute would gather she needed help and had a potential mental disability.

So I again sent her to Social Security, which was close by, she again was sent away. I then called the manager for that office, who was known to us, and asked that he speak to their front desk staff to be on the lookout for her and to see that she was seen based on disability. Again she was sent away and did not return to see me. Later her landlord called to speak to me, I had spoken to him before assuring him of some intervention, letting me know she wasn't willing to see anyone else, as no one would help her. He had been letting her slide for months on the rent as she had such obvious problems, but felt he couldn't do this any further. I asked him to get her to a clinic to get a diagnosis and again send her to Social Security. I never knew what ultimately happened to this poor lady and was furious with the Social Security Office for not accommodating her. There are some people that require that we work around normal procedures to get them some help. Unfortunately, there are employees everywhere who will not do this.

To other issues. Oh, there is light at end of tunnel. Someone wants to transfer in, as we are considered a desirable office. Oh no, transfer is known to be a problem. So I had someone call, as a friend, to advise them not to transfer to my unit as I was too difficult, liked to fire. It worked, didn't need that problem worker.

CHAPTER SIX

NEW DIGS

Let me tell you from my perspective, commonly shared by coworkers, an insider's view of the welfare system and the recipients. First, it is necessary to speak of the most negatively viewed group: those who do not work and are not elderly or disabled. Generally they have never worked and never been married, at least to someone who works. Now Barack Obama will tell you that there is no one who doesn't want to work; this is so untrue. But he comes from Chicago, the birthplace of Urban Studies. Urban Studies is a real light-weight in higher education, more interested in race than other issues and highlighting supporting statistics while poo-pooing others. He also comes from a Job's Program background, which pays some people, in a very ineffectual way, to become acquainted with the work concept.

Sorry, but I digressed, in fairness, some clients have never been closely associated, i.e., socialized, with anyone who did work. Work is not part of their life's experience. Grandma didn't work, Mother didn't work, Auntie didn't work, Daddy only came and went. At one time this was a black issue, but has increasingly become a white issue. When it becomes OK not to work, people don't. Worse, people—yes, government money is actually money from the people—will give them money if they don't work. Many think those who work are worse than stupid. Also, many who never worked for other than minimum wage can realistically see no financial benefit. Why is this difficult to understand?

What really epitomizes this explanation is to see the reaction when a client is told, no they can't get any money, or later, with the Jobs Program in play, they must start a training program, school, or work. Screaming, yelling, threats, hyperventilation ensues. It's like being around Redd Fox when he's having his heart attacks, oh so much drama. Changing from the old welfare system, where you could not suggest a client seek employment at peril of losing your own job, to the Jobs Program, where you had to insist a client seek employment also at peril of losing your own job should you not do so, clearly delineated the embeddings of a deep nonwork culture. After decades of never being able to tell people to work, we relished the opportunity, for a while. After a few years, we realized the additional benefits in dollars given to get someone to work for a short period of time was more than the welfare check, i.e., day care, transportation, training, etc. Further, it became grueling work to be continually presented with the same clients who had been trained, trained, and retrained…to no avail, losing job after job, more quickly than one would think possible.

One aspect of welfare reform that we all loved was the pot of money from the Feds that meant "never before dreamed of" renovations. We all got new computers, very nice modern desk setups, file cabinets, bookcases, ergonomic chairs. Offices were repaired, repainted, and recarpeted. Offices were renamed. Programs were renamed. We had workshops and training where coffee and Danishes were provided. We acted more professional, the clients acted more differently also. I was in seventh heaven, I had an office with a door.

But the bubble burst, actually it was the overhead pipes, as welfare buildings were characteristically old. But we cherished our new digs and saved the day by covering everything in line of the impressive pipe leak with plastic tablecloths from past baby showers, etc. It would have been nice if the building owners and our own upper management would have made the effort to acknowledge the tens of thousands or more in savings through our efforts, but for us it was the right thing to do and that was enough.

The other side of the coin on welfare reform was the agency itself. Now we had all the new computers we would have to learn to use them. Basically one or two from each office would learn the welfare benefits computer program apps. So all data then was directly entered by the caseworkers and approved to directly generate benefits. Before this it was all paperwork generated to teleprocessing departments. Learning all this and then returning to our offices to teach and authorize usage really separated the wheat from the chaff in supervision, likewise for the caseworkers, and maybe more so. Some simply could not make the transition.

It really was a great expectation to believe that caseworkers who had dealt with three copy NCR forms for a few years or maybe twenty years should be able to transition to direct systems entry of thirty, forty, fifty, or more computer screens for each client and further know when the outcome is the correct one, and if not where to look for possible entry errors. However, this was the expectation. No pay raise either. A few people recognized they couldn't make the transition and retired, quit, or took demotions. But this was not the common reaction. Who could really blame them? So there was a lot of open hostility.

A good example of not making it was the supervisor, Miss IKAP, who after six months or so couldn't even handle signing in. This meant if a worker needed an online approval, they would have to first help her sign in. Often this also meant a call to the help desk for a password reset, as she seldom remembered hers. Thank God, she actually retired after treading water for it seemed ever. We also had Social Services workers who really only needed to enter in record comments, which was one direct-entry screen, who couldn't handle that after two years.

All this only emphasizes how much the rest of us adapted and excelled. Without those adapting, there would have been lots of people with no checks, food stamps, or Medicaid. In other words, a fiasco.

In preparation for yet another cataclysm of change, supervisory staff was switched around to other offices, in order that there would be a fair mix of expertise in food stamps, cash (ADC), Medicaid, JOBS, day care, etc. Due to changes in welfare laws, clients were to be required, unless disabled or aged, to GET A JOB or go to school until they could GET A JOB. Remember that song, we often would be humming it triumphantly. This meant caseworkers needed to be all things to clients, including find the right bus routes to that job interview, if called upon to do so. Day care was huge, everyone seemed to get day care vouchers except for the client who took the short courses to become day care providers. In that case they were on the receiving end of day care vouchers. On a personal level this really set me off as the politically connected prima donna in the training department couldn't do training as she used her work time to do her schoolwork, as she was working towards a master's degree. I also was working on a master's degree while working, but I was not politically connected, so I would have to do her job also. Sour grapes!

But I digressed. Remember I said some were being shifted to other offices. More sour grapes this meant me too. I was sent to another office somewhat more distant from my home, with heavier traffic. How unfair! I had done more than my share for this f—-ing agency. I did behave badly. But I was entitled to a reasonable period of hissy fits. This gave me a 110-mile trip two to three days a week including school. They needed a Medicaid expert and that meant me. This exposed me to new riches of personalities and situational dramas.

First day at new site. Introductions ensue to other supervisors and staff. Strangely, Mrs. B as in Bible states her name and says my colors are white and gold. I'm like, is this a uniform exclusive to you, not to be worn by others? Do others here have their colors? Note Mrs. B did have on that day her colors and on most of all days to come. OMG. The lunchroom was not available during lunch as BIBLE STUDIES prevailed. Was this not a government agency with separation of powers? Oh, I did complain. It did end. Now Bible Studies was moved to a supervisor's office, which became a tight squeeze. In re Mrs. B, it is also to be said that others shared with me that whereas she did dress rather expensively, it was possible to do so as she never removed the tags so she could return them after a few wearings. Interesting. She also seemed to have an incredibly short work day. Can't say when she came or went, but I never remember seeing her after say, lunch. She taught a class at a local community college.

Another person of interest, Miss your butt is hanging out of your running shorts (for the purpose of brevity—Miss Butt, no really Cheeks, just Cheeks) was someone soon to be promoted in the stated agenda of having management reflect the ethnicity of the clients (now referred to as customers as our new director was an old Motor City exec). The nomenclature, customer, was one of the few accomplishments (?) of his time of service. Sorry, I have sold him short, he also provided better settings for our workshops and, perhaps, a chocolate chip cookie.

I believe the second time she was present in one of our meetings, she, rather appallingly, was screaming and pounding on our bosses desk, in an effort to impress us all with her excitement with the new JOBS program. This along with the fact she would change before leaving work and run through the office with, you got it, her cheeks hanging out of her running shorts. This could not be missed as when she ran, even then, made such a din, bam, bam, bam. Whereas she did have a modicum of knowledge and dressed rather well, but in an in-your-face look, no that is too generous, she really belonged working with longshore men.

There is yet one other supervisor of note. Along with me and our boss, she was the only white face, aside from myself and one new caseworker, who will become infamous. Whereas my boss and I could fit into this setting, she was entirely, in all ways, completely "white bread." For this reason she is known to me as Mainstreet. Mainstreet was begrudging of every dime government or taxpayer spent, but was truly bent out of shape for every day care voucher she had to print. Her specific value to this office was meant to be that she knew day care regulations. The truth was she didn't want to follow them, but make personal judgment calls. No day passed that she didn't go into a full tilt rant on the unfairness of her paying day care for her kids and "these people" getting it for free. It was entertaining, but did grow old, I swear she would have been very at home wearing the US flag as a blouse while attending a Trump rally. No, she really belonged on FOX as a Judge Jeanine replacement. Come to think of it, she also spoke in a rather loud monotone. I can only imagine how she would react to illegals crossing the Southern border. She was as out of place as a blue M&M.

Now we really have to talk about a very special person, who was an exception to all rules. No, she was actually without rules. In another setting, I could have had some empathy for her, but not here. Rumor said she was the niece of a highest level county executive. Facial recognition, for me, confirmed this, as did the intervening phone calls. For this reason I knew her as Dead Ringer. She was the epitome of entitled elitist. Sadly, she had not a modicum of applicable skills or ability to learn. She had worked in the venerable JOBS Department, which was now, for good reason, defunct. There she could have hid. But as a caseworker with an assigned load, if you didn't do your job people didn't eat, get a check, a medical card, and on and on. These same people would justifiably complain.

Know this, she did go through weeks of formal training and was not expected to walk in and, unassisted, see clients and provide or end benefits. Fortunately, my unit had several very helpful and considerate people. They and I worked with her to see clients and never were given the impression, by her, that she did not understand, except for an incredibly vacuous look. When someone was not actively sitting beside her, she would simply stare at the black computer screen, If advised a client was waiting to see her, she would just continue to sit and stare at the computer screen. Sometimes with a client at her desk, she would walk off with no reason or valid purpose, until someone hunted her down.

She also, on one occasion, simply left a client sitting at her desk, and went home, or God knows where. Clients would call or show up crying to see me as they were that frustrated. They knew that she knew not and never would. I began writing her up, and behold a person from a disabilities group was assigned to her full time as an occupational therapist for two weeks, which became a month or more. He left, only to return again. By this time I worked for the agency for more than twenty years. In that time I do not recall anyone having their own, at county expense, onsite occupational therapist. He finally told me that not only would she never be able to do the job, but she also was a frequent liar. I let him know I agreed, but ability to remove her might require that he actively worked on this with me. That got him removed ever so quickly.

The other caseworkers who were helping to keep client benefits rolling complained. I wrote her up diligently to no avail, my boss was told that she's a genius and we were all lacking. She had done ever so well in college, I'm sure with many advantages for her disability, which remained unnamed. Finally, I threw down and let my boss know to call the director to get the OK to remove going over HR's head or I would put his neglect of this duty in writing with copy to director. In the morning she was gone, still with the agency, still getting caseworker pay but in a spot she could do little damage. No problem when an administrator has a relative who needs money and that person can reasonably do a job, but otherwise please don't throw the whole system in a turmoil. Instead write them a check, buy them a car, pay for school, let them live in your basement. I'm sure what I did ruffled a few feathers, but those immediately around me breathed a lot easier. Certainly a few hundred clients got what they were entitled to in a timely manner.

CHAPTER SEVEN

HALLELUJAH FISH BACK IN WATER

Well, it seems I had done the job I came for and was able to return to an office closer to home. This was considered a personal favor from the acting director, but I didn't consider it so, as I shouldn't have been moved to begin with. Generally speaking, this office was a bore in comparison. Yes, there were incidents, getting settled in and adapting to a new office and unit. One thing worth mentioning to show you how much of a control freak some can be. Everyone in this office—caseworkers and supervisors—had bookcases. You really needed them as we had volumes of the Public Assistant Manual, Food Stamp Manual, Referral Directories to other agencies, etc. I however, had none and supervisors needed them more than caseworkers. So one was moved into my office from a vacant worker's cubicle, of which there were several. This was met with a hissy fit of mammoth proportions from the Center Director, which was a job with high pay and nondescript purpose added under the JOBS initiative, perhaps an effort to use up federal funds rather than lose them.

Her reasoning was that if and when the worker spot was filled they wouldn't have a bookcase. Well, I didn't have one right now, she actually had a clerk remove my manuals from that bookcase and return it to its original setting. I made a call as I wasn't going to start there being treated like a stepchild. The Center Director must have gotten a phone call, as she actually had her secretary empty her bookcase and move it to my office and load my manuals in it. What a pissing contest. I just didn't want to start as a stepchild.

My next incident of note involved another worker in my new unit that also had a disability that made it very difficult to do his job. Again, he previously was in the Jobs Department where he could have worked, but our jobs were too difficult in knowledge and volume for him. I felt very bad for him, again a relative of a politician, in this case, he felt embarrassed, but knew this was too much for him and voluntarily took a lesser job. Sometimes the relatives are well meaning, but doing the wrong thing for agency and their own relative.

At some point in my agency experience, a Commissioner actually did the right thing to get a feeling what our jobs entailed. He visited our office and sat in with worker/client interviews, seeing spontaneous benefits issued or denied, observing difficulty occurring in online entry and approvals. He was very impressed and left with an entirely different view of what our jobs entailed.

I should note that in Texas and one other state, in an effort to save money and have a more accurate job done, the states turned over some part of the agency's work to private companies, this lasted two months as the companies said the work was too complicated to be done by those they had hired and also not enough money for the complexity of the work.

Another funny little tale to tell involved onsite training held by then a state trainer, who I knew from some years ago and had been work friends with until she left under unusual circumstances. The director asked my boss if I would please help with this training. It went fine for a few days. We were working fine together, although she was quite weak in a few areas. After lunch the third day or so, I was sitting next to a good-looking young man, who asked me to clarify something. As I knew him rather well we were giggling about something. OMG, it was like I poked the hornet's nest. The end of the day I was called into my boss's office to say the director wanted me out of the training as I was being disruptive and belittling the trainer's roll. I, of course, was asked what this was all about. I chose not to explain, as it seemed too ridiculous.

You see, that trainer, Mrs. Confused, then a middle-aged, rather pretty, married black woman had been telling me how she had the hots for the young man I just mentioned. I had let her know that he was indeed good-looking and fun, but very much an out of the closet gay, younger, white man, when that still was frowned on. She was simply incensed that she thought that I was putting the moves on him, which was ridiculous. The following day the director stopped and called me into the office to apologize for pulling me out of the training, Mrs. Confused was sent back to the state, never to be heard of or seen again. It seems someone complained about her and further the story may have leaked back to him. And yes would I go back and do the training until they could get a replacement, which I reluctantly did. So much drama. With all this drama, work was not a bore.

This takes me to yet another out of the closet situation. There was another supervisor in that office that I knew and was friends with since early in my employment. He was always fun so we did speak a lot. In fact another person asked me rather bluntly, if we had something going on. I laughed out loud about this, as though he was cute, I knew him long enough that he was like a little brother to me. Little did we know, he was hot after this other very attractive lady, Flame, who I also was very friendly with. As it happened I asked her to stop at my house as I had several good suits that I knew I would never get into again and felt they would fit her. What a revelation.

After trying on a few things, Flame and I sat down for some coffee, I started to get a few strange feelings that something was going to jump out of Pandora's box. And they did. Flame shared with me that she was bisexual and further that she found me very attractive. How did I feel about that? Surprised as I was quite a bit older and I may have thought she might be other than thoroughly straight, but never had a clue I was her prey. Worse I thought poor Alvin, my friend, was totally barking up the wrong tree. So I made clear I only was interested in through-and-through heterosexuals, but thank you for showing an interest and I will show you to the door.

I think it's time to leave. I'm thinking retiring is best while my mind still functions. It's been interesting, fun at times, heartbreaking, and an evolution of mind and spirit. But it's time to leave, becoming too automated, too regimented, and rigid. I'm leaving while the good old days are not a too-distant memory. To those who stayed, good luck. Do please leave before becoming a joke or a cynic. I hope I have. I hope I have helped some very deserving and overlooked souls. Before I say too much, goodbye.

Printed in the USA
CPSIA information can be obtained
at www.ICGtesting.com
LVHW021557080824
787585LV00014B/424